**'I suppos**
**consider re**

'Repeating the event?' She stared at him, wondering if he meant purely to fool his friends again. 'I'm not sure we could keep up the pretence for too long—I'm sure someone would suspect.'

'I wasn't meaning keeping up any pretence,' he said softly. 'I was thinking more about you and I getting to know one another properly.'

She stared at him, hardly able to believe what she was hearing, then, as an expression of pure tenderness came into his eyes, she felt her pulse begin to race.

'Would you like that, Lara?' he asked. Reaching out his hand, he gently touched her cheek.

'Yes,' she whispered. 'Yes, Andres, I would.'

**Laura MacDonald** was born and bred in the Isle of Wight, where she still lives with her husband. The Island is a place of great natural beauty and forms the backdrop for many of Laura's books. She has been writing fiction since she was a child. Her first book was published in the 1980s, and she has been writing full time since 1991, during which time she has produced over forty books for both adults and children. When she isn't writing her hobbies include painting, reading and researching family history.

**Recent titles by the same author:**

THE POLICE DOCTOR'S DISCOVERY
THE DOCTOR'S SPECIAL CHARM
*(Eleanor James Memorial Hospital)*
A VERY SPECIAL SURGEON
*(Eleanor James Memorial Hospital)*
MEDITERRANEAN RESCUE
UNDER SPECIAL CARE
*(Eleanor James Memorial Hospital)*

# THE LATIN SURGEON

BY

LAURA MACDONALD

MILLS & BOON®

*First published in Great Britain 2005*
*Harlequin Mills & Boon Limited,*
*Eton House, 18-24 Paradise Road, Richmond, Surrey TW9 1SR*



ISBN 0 263 84298 3

*Set in Times Roman 10½ on 12 pt.*
*03-0405-48365*

*Printed and bound in Spain*
*by Litografia Rosés, S.A., Barcelona*

## CHAPTER ONE

THE first time she saw him was on a cold January day when the wind chill made it feel far colder than the actual temperature. Dressed in a long, black overcoat and wearing a black fedora, he was walking briskly along a stretch of pavement towards the hospital, but at that time, of course, Lara had no idea who he was. She was in her car, also approaching the hospital, and within a matter of seconds had overtaken him. As she signalled to turn right into the hospital grounds, he caught up with her. She turned, imagining he would stop and wait for her, but to her dismay he appeared not to have seen her and, with his head down against the wind, carried on walking. With a muttered expletive Lara slammed on her brakes, bringing the car to a halt with a squeal of tyres only inches away from the man.

He stopped short, turning towards her and raising his hands, the gesture a mixture of shock, maybe briefly anger, then irritation as he stepped back onto the kerb to allow her to pass. Very briefly her gaze met his, and beneath the brim of the hat she was aware of olive skin, liquid dark eyes and strong, hawk-like features. With a slight inclination of his head he indicated for her to pass him. Afterwards she was to wonder what it had been about him that had attracted her attention in the first place—the way he moved perhaps, the fact that he was a stranger unknown to her, or maybe it had been his attire. There weren't too many men of her acquaintance who wore black fedoras. But at the time she was more concerned with the fact that she had almost run him over, and that she was slightly late and needed to move smartly if she was to be on time for report.

By the time she had parked her car in the area assigned to the burns unit of St Joseph's hospital, locked it and entered the unit by the staff entrance, there was no sign of the stranger. No doubt he was a visitor, or maybe a patient with an appointment. Unwinding her scarf and pulling off her gloves, Lara hurried into the staff changing room where she found her friend and fellow staff nurse Katie Soames, who had already changed into her uniform and was about to leave for the wards.

'Oh, there you are,' said Katie. 'I was beginning to think you weren't coming.'

'I know.' Lara pulled a face. 'I'm late. Luke wanted some last-minute help with his homework.'

'The kids are OK?' Katie looked faintly anxious, no doubt remembering the many problems Lara faced.

'Oh, yes.' Lara nodded. 'They're fine.' She looked frantically around then reached out and touched the doorframe. 'Touch wood,' she added hastily. 'Whenever I say something like that, there is another crisis.' She didn't mention the two bills that had arrived that morning—the bills they weren't sure how they were going to pay. 'Anyway,' she went on, 'I must get changed—you go on. Cover for me if you can—I'll be with you in a couple of minutes.' As the door closed behind Katie, Lara quickly pulled off her coat then her jumper and jeans, replacing them with the smart tunic and tapered trousers she wore on the unit. Pausing in front of the mirror just long enough to draw her unruly mass of auburn curls back from her face and twist them into a band, she hurried from the changing rooms.

Once on the large, open-plan ward with its central nursing station and four-bedded bays, Lara quickly made her way into the ward sister's office where the morning report had just got under way. Sue Jackman raised her eyebrows at Lara but made no comment about the fact that she was late, while Lara mouthed the single word 'Sorry' and slipped as unobtrusively as possible onto a chair at the back of the room. Desperately she tried to focus her mind and concentrate on what the night sister was telling Sister Jackman and the rest of the day staff.

A patient had been transferred to the burns unit during the night from St Joseph's accident and emergency unit with severe burns to his chest and arms following a fire at his home started by a smouldering cigarette. Two other patients were scheduled for Theatre that morning for skin grafts following burns, while the remainder of the patients on the ward were in various stages of recovery from burns sustained in accidents.

'What you may not be aware of this morning,' said Sue, looking round at her staff over the top of her glasses, 'is that following Mr Sylvester's heart attack a locum has had to be found at very short notice to take his place.'

'So have they got someone?' asked Katie.

'Apparently, yes,' Sue replied. 'His name…' she consulted the papers in her hand '…is Mr Ricardo and he is a plastic surgeon in a private clinic in London, but he does locum work from time to time.'

'Sounds interesting,' said Katie. 'Do you know anything about him?'

'No, I don't.' Sue shook her head. 'His name sounds

Spanish but, no doubt, we'll find out soon. He'll be along shortly to see the two patients who are due for grafts today.'

When report was over Lara made her way onto the ward where she had been assigned the task of preparing one of the two patients who were to have surgery that morning. The patient's name was Jennifer Reece and she had suffered disfiguring burns to her face in a fire at her home. Her wounds had been treated on the unit following the accident and a skin graft had been discussed and agreed on with John Sylvester, the consultant surgeon attached to the burns unit.

'So are you saying it won't be Mr Sylvester doing the operation?' Jennifer Reece looked at Lara in consternation after hearing that Mr Sylvester was not available.

'That's right.' Lara nodded. 'Mr Sylvester unfortunately is sick at the moment but I understand a locum has been found to take his place.'

'I'm not sure I like the sound of that,' said Jennifer anxiously. 'It's taken a lot of courage for me to agree to this skin graft in the first place.'

'Yes,' Lara replied sympathetically, 'I can imagine, and I know you must be very disappointed, but—'

'So who is this new man?' Jennifer interrupted. 'What do you know about him?'

'Well,' Lara admitted, 'I don't know anything much at all at the moment except that he works at a clinic in London that specialises in cosmetic surgery.'

'I don't like the sound of that,' said Jennifer in alarm. 'I've heard about those clinics—there are a lot of cowboys running those places—you hear all sorts of stories about things going wrong…'

'You mustn't worry about that,' said Lara, seeking

to reassure her patient. 'If St Joseph's has engaged the services of this man as a locum, you can rest assured that he is highly qualified and that his work is of the highest standard. St Joseph's has a reputation to maintain.'

'Even so, I think I would rather wait until Mr Sylvester comes back,' Jennifer persisted.

'I don't think that's a good idea.'

'Why not?' Jennifer demanded. 'He is coming back, isn't he?'

'Well, we certainly hope so,' Lara replied, 'but he has been very ill and it will take him some considerable time to recuperate. I honestly think, Jennifer, that you would be well advised to let this operation go ahead as planned.'

'Well, I don't know...'

'Look, Sister tells me that this new man is coming onto the ward shortly to meet you and another patient who is going to Theatre today. Why don't you wait until after you have met him before you make any final decision?'

'Well...all right, then.' Jennifer still sounded extremely doubtful but at least Lara had persuaded her not to discharge herself from the ward. For the next quarter of an hour Lara completed the paperwork necessary before any operation, checking Jennifer's medication and history of previous illnesses and operations, only stopping short at the actual consent signature.

'I'm sure the surgeon will be here soon,' she said as she gathered up the papers. Glancing at Jennifer, she realised that she wasn't listening, that her attention had been taken by something going on at the entrance to the bay. Turning her head to see what Jennifer was looking at, she realised that Sue Jackman had come into the bay and that a man accompanied her.

'Is that him now?' asked Jennifer.

'I don't know…' Lara began, then stopped. 'Oh,' she said as something about the man struck a chord. He was tall, and at first glance his head appeared shaven, but a closer look revealed that his dark hair was cropped very, very close to his head. He wore dark clothes, a jacket and trousers over a black polo-neck shirt. The last time she'd seen him he'd been wearing a black fedora and a long overcoat, but there was no mistaking those liquid dark eyes or that hawk-like profile. She had almost run him over, she thought in sudden dismay as it dawned on her that the new locum and the man who had stepped out in front of her car that very morning were one and the same person.

'Mrs Reece.' Sue was talking and Lara attempted to concentrate, but for some reason found it difficult under the slightly aloof gaze of the surgeon. 'This is Mr Ricardo. We are extremely fortunate that he has been able to come to St Joseph's at such short notice to step into Mr Sylvester's shoes.'

'Mrs Reece.' The surgeon inclined his head in the patient's direction then briefly turned to Lara who was still scrabbling with her papers.

'Oh, sorry,' Sue continued. 'This is Staff Nurse Lara Gregory.'

'Actually,' said the surgeon, his eyes like two black pools, 'we have already met…'

'Really?' said Sue in surprise.

'Or rather I should say we have encountered one another,' he corrected himself. 'Staff Nurse Gregory almost ran me over this morning even before I had set foot in the hospital—I think it fair to say she was in something of a hurry.'

The implication was clearly that she had been driving too fast and Lara felt herself flush. 'I doubt it would have happened had you been looking where you were going,' she retorted crisply.

For one moment there was silence then a startled Sue hastened to defuse the sudden tension, which to her must have appeared to erupt out of nowhere. 'Is all the paperwork completed, Nurse Gregory?' she asked crisply.

'No,' Lara replied. 'Mrs Reece isn't at all certain that she wants an unknown surgeon to perform her skin graft—she had been counting on it being done by Mr Sylvester.' She could hardly believe she had said that—under normal circumstances in such a situation she would have been far more discreet, especially in front of a locum surgeon, but there had been something about this man that had antagonised her with his implication that she had been speeding when, in actual fact, it had been entirely his own fault for not looking before he'd stepped into the road. She was aware of Sue's horrified glance but suddenly she didn't care.

'Maybe Mrs Reece and myself should have a little talk.' Mr Ricardo pulled a chair forward so that he could sit beside Jennifer. As Sue and Lara would have moved away, he lifted one hand. 'Please, stay, Nurse Gregory,' he said. 'Maybe you need to hear this as well.'

For the second time that morning Lara felt the colour rise to her face.

* * *

'So what happened?' It was later in the morning and Katie had waylaid Lara by the nurses' station. 'Sue said Jennifer Reece was at the point of refusing surgery.'

'She was,' Lara agreed. 'But our new locum charmed her to such an extent that by the time he had finished she was practically eating out of his hand.'

'What did he say?'

'Well, he started by giving her all the low-down on his qualifications and his background then he talked about her injuries, examined her facial wounds and the donor site on her thigh and gave her a step-by-step guide to the procedure he would use during the actual graft, then he explained what her recovery period would involve and what she can expect in time.'

'And all that swayed her?'

'Must have done.' Lara shrugged. 'She's in Theatre now.'

'So what's all this about you having a go at him?' asked Katie curiously.

'I didn't have a go at him,' Lara protested. 'Well, not exactly.'

'Sue said you did—she didn't sound too happy about it. She said there she was, trying to be helpful to him on his first morning, and you attacked him—and in front of a patient as well.'

'I didn't attack him!'

'So what was it all about?' Katie clearly wasn't going to let the matter drop. 'Sue said he'd given the impression that the pair of you had already met. I didn't know you'd met him.' She sounded faintly accusing. 'You never said anything.'

'That was because I *hadn't* actually met him,' Lara protested. 'At least, I didn't know who he was.'

'So what happened?' asked Katie. She appeared more curious than ever.

'He stepped out in front of my car, that's what,' said Lara. 'He quite simply wasn't looking where he was going and then afterwards he had the nerve to suggest it had been my fault—that I had been driving too fast.'

'And were you?' asked Katie mildly.

'What?'

'Driving too fast?'

'No, of course I wasn't,' she protested.

'When was this exactly?'

'This morning, before I started my shift.'

'When you were late?'

Lara stared at her friend. 'Look,' she said, 'whose side are you on?'

'Sorry,' said Katie with a grin. 'I'm sure you weren't driving too fast. I'm sure it was all that nasty Mr Ricardo's fault.'

'Yes, well...'

'Talking of him, where is he from exactly? You said you heard all about his background—is he Spanish?'

'Actually,' Lara replied, 'he's from Buenos Aires—he told Jennifer Reece his mother is English but his father is from Argentina and that's where he's been living and working.'

'Hmm, interesting,' said Katie thoughtfully. 'What did you think of him?'

'I don't know enough about him to form an opinion yet,' said Lara with a shrug.

'OK, first impressions, then—apart from nearly killing him, of course.'

'He seems rather aloof.' Lara wrinkled her nose. 'Almost as if he's on some lofty pinnacle far removed from the rest of us mere mortals.'

'So you didn't fancy him, then?' Katie gave a wicked grin.

'Fancy him? No, of course not. He's not my type,' she added lightly. 'I prefer blond men with blue eyes.'

'I thought he was rather yummy,' said Katie.

'You would,' said Lara with a sniff.

'Thank you, Dr Martin, that is looking very neat. I'm sure the lady will be pleased. If I can leave you to finish…' Andres Ricardo glanced at his assistant then moved away from the operating table after completing Jennifer Reece's skin graft. The operation had gone well with the new skin taken from her inner thigh and grafted over the site on her face where she had sustained the worst of her burns. After acknowledging the rest of the operating team, he strode from the theatre, pulling off his mask and cap as he did so. Minutes later he had washed and changed out of his theatre greens and boots and into his day clothes. He returned to the consulting room that had been allocated to him.

Briefly he glanced at a few papers on his desk, then crossed to the window and stared out at the hospital grounds. If he was strictly honest, he still wasn't sure about this locum post, any more than he was completely sure that coming to London and going into partnership with Theo McFarlane and Arun Chopa at the Roseberry Clinic had been the right decision. Outside in the grounds the wind tossed the bare branches of the trees and the grey banks of cloud threatened even more rain. He missed the wide blue skies and the hot sun of his homeland and wished fervently that he was back there, in spite of the fact that Argentina held so many painful memories.

Surely now, after five years, the perpetual ache in his heart that constantly reminded him of Consuela should have subsided a little, but instead of time being the great healer it was supposed to be, if anything the ache had grown worse. In some ways time played strange tricks and diffused the memories, so much so that these days he had to work hard to recall certain details—the softness of her skin as she lay beside him, the way her eyes would flash with laughter or anger, the fall of her thick, dark hair against her sun-kissed shoulders or the gentle curve of her cheek. Sometimes he had to work so hard to recall those things that he would break out in sweat, and in anger and frustration be forced to abandon the attempt. But he mustn't let those memories go, he thought in sudden desperation, they were all he had. Maybe this elusiveness was because he was in a different country. Maybe he shouldn't have been persuaded into coming here—maybe, even now, it wasn't too late to go back.

He had joined the partnership at the Roseberry Clinic at the instigation of his friend and partner, Theo McFarlane, with whom he had trained at medical school and who had gone on to work with him for a time in Buenos Aires. But already he was questioning the move, just as right now he was wondering whether he would live to regret agreeing to the locum work here at St Joseph's. His friends meant well, he knew that, just as he knew that by trying to open up new opportunities for him and presenting him with new challenges, they were trying to help him to move on in his life. What none of them understood was the fact that not only would he never move on from what he'd had with Consuela but that he didn't even want to.

A sudden knock at the door jolted him out of his reverie and caused him to turn sharply. 'Come in,' he called.

The door opened and the staff nurse who had nearly

killed him earlier that day stood on the threshold. 'I've brought you the reports you wanted,' she said. Did her chin tilt ever so defiantly or was he imagining it? She'd been quite abrasive toward him when he'd hinted she'd been driving too fast did she intend to keep up this hostile attitude towards him? Well, if so, that was fine by him, he thought almost angrily. He had far more important things on his mind than whether or not some silly little red-haired nurse was hell-bent on waging some ridiculous vendetta. He still thought she'd been driving too fast, especially when entering hospital grounds.

'Thank you,' he replied tersely. 'Is Mrs Reece back in the ward yet?'

'Yes—will you come and see her before you go?'

'Of course,' he replied. She turned to go and he noticed that her hair was caught up in a black velvet band. Earlier, when he'd first seen her in the car when she had all but flattened him, it had been loose—a wild, fiery cloud. He'd never been attracted to red-haired women—never known many, in fact. Most of the women he'd ever known had been dark, with black hair, olive complexions and dark eyes—just like Consuela…

'I'll be along shortly,' he said, suddenly feeling he needed to say something else, 'and I'll see Mr Freeman as well. Has he come round yet?'

'Yes, I believe so.' She turned and glanced back at him, and he noticed that her eyes were green and her skin pale—creamy almost. 'I believe sister wanted to talk to you about pain control.'

'Very well.' He nodded. 'Thank you, Nurse.'

The door clicked shut behind her and with a sigh he turned back to the window. Should he have said something about earlier? She'd accused him of not looking where he'd been going—had that been true? Probably, he told himself reluctantly. No doubt once again he'd been deeply immersed in thoughts of Consuela and had been totally unaware of what had been going on around him. But that didn't alter the fact that she had been driving too fast in the first place.

'What was all that about on the ward this morning?'

Lara was nearing the end of her shift when Sue waylaid her. 'All what?' she asked with a little sigh, knowing full well what the sister was referring to.

'All that between you and Mr Ricardo—about you nearly running him over. Was it true?'

'Yes, actually, it was.' Lara nodded. 'Like I said at the time, he wasn't looking where he was going.'

'Well, maybe he wasn't, but did you have to react quite so strongly, and on his first day at that?' asked Sue.

'He as good as accused me of speeding,' Lara declared hotly.

'And you weren't?' Sue raised one eyebrow.

'Of course not,' Lara retorted. 'Well, I might have been,' she added, catching Sue's rather sceptical expression. 'Just a little bit. But I still say he should have looked before stepping onto the road. Let's face it, Sue, if I'd hit him and he'd been injured or, heaven forbid, killed, I would have got the blame.'

'Yes, I don't doubt that,' said Sue, 'but I just feel it was a shame that you got off to such a bad start with him. After all, he's going to be around quite a bit if he's taking Mr Sylvester's place.'

'Yes, I suppose…' Lara shrugged.

'And from what I've heard about him he's good—very good. We were actually very lucky to get him.'

'Yes, I don't doubt it,' Lara said. 'All right, Sue,' she added, when it appeared that the ward sister was waiting for her to say something further, 'I'll do my best to get on with him—for the sake of the unit.'

'Right, Lara,' Sue said briskly. 'You know how much store I set by the smooth running of this place.'

'Yes, Sue, I know you do.' Lara glanced up as a tall figure came through the double doors onto the wards. 'Uh-oh,' she said, 'speak of the devil…'

For a moment it seemed as if he knew they had been talking about him as he glanced from Sue to Lara then back to Sue again.

'Mr Ricardo,' said Sue, 'can we help you? I thought you would have gone by now.'

'I would like to take a look at the two skin-graft patients before I go,' he said.

'Oh, right, very well.' Sue sounded surprised. It was unusual to say the least for the surgeon to come back onto the ward unless there had been any complications during surgery. 'Lara…' she half turned '…would you take Mr Ricardo onto the ward, please?'

Lara wanted to refuse, to say that her shift was all but over, that she was in a hurry, had Callum to pick up from school, but somehow, in the light of their recent conversation, she didn't quite dare. 'Of course,' she heard herself murmur dutifully. 'If you'd like to come with me, Mr Ricardo.'

Without a word he fell into step beside her and together they entered one of the ward's four-bedded bays. Jennifer was recovering in the bed nearest the entrance, her face covered in dressings.

'Hello, Mrs Reece—Jennifer.' The surgeon went

right up to her and leaned over the bed. 'Are you comfortable?'

'Oh, yes,' she said, realising who her visitor was. 'Yes, thank you, Mr Ricardo.'

'No pain?' he asked gently.

'Not really. My leg actually feels more tender than my face, if I'm honest.'

'It is very often the case,' he replied, 'that the donor site is more painful than the recipient site. But we can give you something for the pain...' He half turned to Lara but Jennifer interrupted.

'Oh, it's all right,' she said. 'Sister gave me an injection about ten minutes ago—I'm just waiting for it to work.'

'Good.' He nodded. 'Your operation went very well, Jennifer,' he said in the same gentle tone. Lara presumed that his faint accent was Spanish—the language spoken in Argentina. 'I was very satisfied with the graft and I hope you will be also,' he went on. 'I am also very optimistic that there will be minimum scarring of both your face and your thigh.'

'Thank you,' said Jennifer, and Lara saw tears well up in the eye that was not covered by the gauze dressings that masked the other side of her face. 'Thank you so much. Mr Ricardo?' she said, when he would have moved away.

'Yes?' He paused at the side of the bed and looked down at his patient.

'I'm sorry I caused such a fuss earlier about who was to do my skin graft.'

'Think no more of it,' he said softly. 'It was quite understandable that you should feel apprehensive. After all, you had never set eyes on me before in your life—how could you be expected to trust your face to me?'

Suddenly Lara felt her own emotions rise dangerously close to the surface. Was this apology time? Maybe she, too, should apologise for having nearly killed this man. Maybe, just maybe, she had been driving just a teeny bit faster than she should have been. On the other hand, maybe it wasn't a good idea to get carried away by the emotional tide that was very often present at the bedside of a patient. And then, before she had the chance to think more on the subject, he had moved away from the bed and she was escorting him to another bay where they found that the second patient to receive a skin graft that day was sleeping.

'Don't disturb him,' Mr Ricardo said quietly. 'I shall be back here in a couple of days' time—I'll see him then.'

And then it was over. The surgeon returned to his consulting room after solemnly thanking Lara, and she came off her shift and hurried to the changing rooms to change out of her uniform and into her day clothes. An anxious glance at the clock told her that she would have to hurry if she was to be at the school in time to pick up Callum. Pulling the band from her hair, she thankfully shook it free then stepped out of her trousers and tunic and pulled on her sweater and jeans. Within moments she was out of the building and hurrying through the grounds to the car park.

It was still cold and very windy, and to make matters even worse it had started to rain. Lara didn't mind wind—in fact, she quite liked a walk when it was windy, enjoying the feel of the wind on her face and through her hair. She didn't really mind the rain either, providing it was of the soft and gentle variety. What she couldn't abide was the wind and rain together just as it was now, when it came in great gusts, stinging the face and drenching her in a matter of minutes. Once in her car she gave a sigh of relief and slammed the door behind her then immediately started the engine and switched on the windscreen wipers.

Her journey through the hospital grounds to the main entrance was uneventful but as she turned onto the road she suddenly caught sight of a familiar figure. Hunched against the rain and battling the wind, dressed once again in the long, black overcoat and with one hand holding on to the black fedora, Andres Ricardo was striding along the pavement by the iron railings that formed the hospital boundary.

At least he's on the pavement and not on the road, thought Lara as she passed him. No fear of running him down this time. She glanced in her rear-view mirror. He looked cold and, no doubt, quite soon in this rain he would be wet through as well. But she couldn't stop—could she? She was in too much of a hurry. He'd be going to the station—she'd heard him telling Sue that he'd come down on the train. And the station was on her way to Callum's school.

She indicated and pulled in to the side of the road. Within seconds he'd drawn alongside her. Leaning across, she wound down the window on the passenger side. 'Are you going to the station?' she asked.

'Yes,' he replied, his expression one of surprise.

'Would you like a lift?'

'That is most kind.' Opening the car door, he somehow folded his tall frame into the passenger seat of her car, slammed the door and fastened his seat belt.

Almost with a sense of disbelief at what she had done, Lara signalled and drew away from the kerb.

# CHAPTER TWO

ANDRES couldn't believe Lara had stopped and offered him a lift, not after what had happened that morning. As they drew away from the kerb he threw her a curious sidelong glance. The black velvet band had gone now and once again her hair was loose—that fiery cloud around her head against the rich, creamy texture of her skin. Her colouring, while not of the type that had attracted him in the past, he found somewhat to his surprise fascinated him now, probably because of the strong contrast between her and the women from home.

'This is very good of you,' he said at last, breaking the silence between them, which was threatening to become embarrassing.

'Not at all,' she replied crisply. 'The weather's dreadful and, besides, I pass the station on the way to the school.'

'You have a child to pick up?' he asked.

'Yes.' She gave a short laugh. 'Then half an hour later his brother and sister from another school.'

'I see.' He paused, finding himself wondering for some reason if she was a single mother. 'This is a busy life you lead.'

'Yes,' she replied, 'it is.' She fell silent again and quite suddenly he felt compelled to say something, anything, about that morning. After all, she hadn't had to stop to give him a lift and in the circumstances it was surprising that she had. He would have thought it much more likely for her to have left him to battle it out against the wind and the rain.

He cleared his throat. 'About earlier…' he began.

'What about earlier?' Her voice was sharper and she half turned her head as if once again she was preparing to go on the defensive.

'I'm willing to admit I may not have been concentrating as much as I should have been,' he said at last. There, he'd said it now. A second glance in her direction saw her chin tilt in that defiant way it had earlier on the ward, and he braced himself for a fresh onslaught as she berated him anew. To his surprise, however, she drew in her breath sharply.

'And I may have been going a little faster than I should have been,' she said.

'Shall we call it quits?' he said lightly.

'If you like.' She gave a little shrug of her shoulders and he suddenly caught the scent of the perfume she was wearing, not a heavy, expensive scent of the type he was used to, but a light, fresh, floral fragrance which for some reason reminded him of fields of summer flowers beneath blue skies.

'Have you been at the burns unit long?' he asked after a while.

'Three years,' she replied. 'Before that I worked in A and E.'

'At St Joseph's?'

'No.' She shook her head. 'At a hospital in Sussex.'

'So why the change to burns?' Suddenly he was curious.

She seemed to hesitate before answering, as if she was wary of letting him know too much about her. 'I became interested in the treatment of burns after a member of my own family was badly burnt in an accident,' she replied at last. Then, almost as if she didn't want any further questions on that subject, she drew the conversation away from herself and onto him. 'What about you?'

'What *about* me?' It was his turn to be wary as he anticipated questions about his private life, questions he wouldn't want to answer. Clenching his hands, he attempted to concentrate on the mesmerising movement of the windscreen wipers.

'Have you been in this country long?' she said.

He relaxed slightly. 'No, not really—only about three months.'

'Did I hear you say earlier you were from Argentina?' she asked.

'Yes,' he said almost reluctantly. 'My home is in a town called Cordoba but I've been working in Buenos Aires at a huge hospital where I specialised in plastic surgery and skin grafts.'

'And you now have a clinic here in London?'

Was there again that tilt of her chin or had he imagined it?

'I am in partnership with two other doctors at the Roseberry Clinic in Chelsea.'

'And this is a private clinic?' she asked.

In the distance through the rain he saw the sign for the station and knew they were almost there. 'Yes,' he replied, 'it is. We deal mainly with cosmetic surgery.'

'Rich women wanting to change the way they look?' she asked. She spoke lightly but Andres detected a slightly mocking edge to her tone.

'Not only that,' he replied. 'Sometimes surgery is carried out for deeply psychological reasons.'

'Such as?'

'The correction of a feature which has caused a patient deep, ongoing distress,' he said, 'or maybe the removal of tattoos, administered in one's youth and causing problems in later life.'

'So are you missing Argentina, Mr Ricardo?' she asked as she brought the car to a halt outside the main entrance to the station.

'I miss the hot sun.' He pulled a face as he peered through the windscreen. 'And the blue skies. It only seems to have rained since I've been here.'

'Oh, we have blue skies, too,' she said as he undid his seat belt and opened the car door. 'Just give it time.'

'Thank you for the lift,' he said as he stood on the pavement, bending his head and holding the door open.

'Don't mention it.'

'And by the way,' he added, 'the name is Andres.'

'OK.' A small smile played around her mouth. 'Mine's Lara.'

He watched her, as with a brief wave of her hand, she drove away then, lifting the collar of his coat, he turned and walked into the station.

Callum couldn't find his coat.

'Here it is,' said Lara. 'Look, it was on someone else's peg.'

'Don't want it on,' said Callum, pulling a face.

'I think you'd better,' Lara replied patiently. 'It's pouring with rain.'

'Does that mean we can't go to the park?' Callum's expression grew anxious.

''Fraid not.'

'But you promised,' Callum wailed.

'I know. I'm sorry, but I didn't know it was going to rain—did I, now?' she added as together they left the school building and hurried across the playground to the school gates.

'S'ppose not,' he said, then added, 'It's *always* raining.'

'I know.' Lara smiled as she realised that Callum's words had echoed the sentiments of her previous passenger. Andres. She hadn't known his first name and it had come as a bit of a surprise when he had told her, almost as if he intended her to use it in future instead of the more formal 'Mr Ricardo.' She wondered briefly what Sue would say if she starting calling him Andres. Sue hated any form of familiarity in front of the patients. Lara had been surprised when he had all but apologised for the incident outside the hospital earlier that day, even going so far as to suggest that it had been his fault for not concentrating. She had been so surprised, in fact, that she'd found herself admitting that she too might have been partly at fault. She hadn't intended saying that, and she didn't really know where it had come from. It was almost as if neither of them wanted to continue any sort of hostility.

'Have we got to pick up Luke and Sophie today?' asked Callum as they reached the car.

'Yes,' Lara replied. 'We have about half an hour to wait—shall we go and buy some sweets while we're waiting?'

'Yes,' Callum said in satisfaction. 'But bags I sit in the front.'

'OK.' Lara opened the passenger door for him.

'Even when we get Luke?' Callum looked up at her.

'Even when we get Luke,' she agreed.

Half an hour later they picked up Luke and Sophie from their school, which was a mile away from Callum's.

'Why's he sitting in the front?' asked Luke, eyeing his younger brother disdainfully.

'Because I said he could,' Lara replied, 'to make up for not being able to go to the park.' She paused. 'Have you got your swimming bag, Sophie?' she asked, her eyes meeting those of the girl in the driving mirror. Sophie was renowned for forgetting things, especially her swimming gear on the days her class went to the local swimming baths.

'Course I have,' said Sophie indignantly. 'Has he got sweets?' She peered over the back of the front seat at her younger brother.

'He has,' said Lara, 'and here are yours.' Bending down, she retrieved two packets of sweets from her bag and passed them back.

'Oh, brill, thanks!' said Sophie.

'Cool,' said Luke.

'What did you say?' said Lara, raising her eyebrows.

'Thanks,' muttered Luke.

A quarter of an hour later they entered the long street of identical terraced houses where they lived and the battle began to find a parking space among the cars parked on either side of the road.

'There's one!' shouted Luke. 'Over there by the tree.'

'Hope I can get into that,' said Lara. 'It doesn't look that big.'

'Yes, you can,' said Luke with all the confidence of his eleven years. 'There's loads of room.'

'OK, Luke.' Lara pulled a face. 'If you say so.'

A few minutes later she had parked successfully between two cars. 'Told you,' said Luke loftily as the children scrambled out of the car, down the pavement and into a house with a tiny front garden and a bright blue front door with a brass doorknocker. Lara followed more slowly and by the time she entered the hallway of the house Luke and Sophie had clattered up the stairs while Callum had made his way into the kitchen at the rear of the house.

It was warm in the kitchen after the damp chill outside, and as Lara pulled off her coat and scarf she called a greeting to the woman sitting at the table onto whose lap Callum had climbed. 'Hi, Cassie, how are things?'

The woman turned her head towards Lara, and as always Lara felt a pang somewhere deep inside as she caught sight of the disfiguring scars across her sister's face and down her neck. 'Not so bad,' she said, but her voice was dull and flat, not full of fun and laughter as it had once been.

'We're making a dinosaur at school,' said Callum suddenly, as if he had just remembered. 'And, Mum,' he went on tugging at the woman's sleeve to make sure he had her attention, 'Lara bought us sweets.'

'Did she?' Cassie hugged him then watched as he slipped from her lap and ran out of the kitchen. 'You spoil them,' she said to Lara, but her words held no accusation, rather gratitude—and not just for buying sweets.

'Well.' Lara gave a little shrug. 'He couldn't go to the park because of the rain and he was so disappointed, and I couldn't buy sweets for him and not for the other two, could I?'

'What sort of a day have you had?' asked Cassie.

Lara considered for a moment. 'Interesting,' she said.

'Oh, in what way?' Cassie stood up and, moving to

the sink, filled the kettle for the inevitable cup of tea she and Lara always shared at this time of day.

'We have a new locum surgeon,'

'Is this to take Mr Sylvester's place?' asked Cassie. She loved to hear about Lara's life at the hospital and about the people she worked with.

'Yes, it is.' Lara took mugs from a cupboard and lifted a china teapot down from a shelf. 'It looks as if Mr Sylvester could be away for some time yet.'

'So in what way was this interesting?' asked Cassie. As she leaned against the sink, the sleeve of her jumper rode up slightly, revealing yet more scars, a reminder that her injuries hadn't only affected her face and neck.

'Well, this new guy isn't the usual run-of-the-mill type. For a start he comes from Argentina, although I believe his mother was English, but I have to say he doesn't look very English.'

'Hopefully he speaks it,' said Cassie.

'Oh, yes, he speaks it very well,' Lara replied, 'and apparently he's very highly qualified. He's also a partner in some private London clinic.'

'Did you get on all right with him?' The switch on the kettle clicked and Cassie turned to fill the teapot. Lara instinctively wanted to step forward to help her, knowing that her sister's vision was impaired, but she knew she mustn't—Cassie's confidence would never be restored if she weren't ever allowed to do things for herself.

'Yes, I suppose so,' Lara replied instead. 'Once he'd got over the fact that I nearly ran him over before he'd even set foot in the hospital. Mind you, I think I more than made up for that by giving him a lift to the station.'

'Sounds as if you got quite friendly with him,' remarked Cassie as she opened the biscuit tin and set out several chocolate biscuits on a plate.

'Not really,' said Lara with a shrug. 'He probably won't even remember who I am the next time I see him—that's the way some of these surgeons are.'

All thoughts of the new surgeon were driven from her mind a moment later as first Luke then Sophie and Callum erupted into the kitchen for the snack and the chat that had recently become something of a daily afternoon ritual.

'Hi, Mum.' Luke dropped a kiss on Cassie's forehead in passing while Sophie lingered for a cuddle from her mother before sitting at the table and reaching out for a biscuit.

For the following half-hour news of the day was exchanged as the children told their mother and Lara what each of them had done at school. With their news over, Lara turned to her sister. 'And what about you?' she said. 'Did the doctor come?'

'Yes, he did.' Cassie held her mug between her hands as if warming them as she sipped her tea. 'He's changed my tablets again,' she added. Then, her eyes meeting Lara's, she added, 'The antidepressants, that is.'

'Well,' said Lara, 'let's hope these will soon make you feel better.'

'I don't like you being sad, Mummy,' said Sophie. 'I want you to be happy and smiley again just like you used to be.'

'I know, darling,' whispered Cassie, the ever-ready tears springing to her eyes. 'So do I.'

'Right,' said Lara, rising to her feet, 'homework time. And, Callum, the guinea pigs' cage needs cleaning out.'

Amid predictable grumbles, the children dispersed and Cassie went upstairs, leaving Lara sitting alone at the kitchen table.

It had been three years now since that terrible day when a pan of hot fat had exploded in Cassie's face, leaving her with severe burns to her face, neck and arms. Three long years of hospital appointments, skin grafts and, for Cassie, debilitating depression, as well as coping with the scarring left from the burns and impaired vision. It had been two years since Cassie's husband Dave had left her, unable to cope with what had happened, and it had been almost two years since Lara had put her own life on hold and moved in with her sister to help care for her and her three children.

It had been a nightmarish time, not only having to deal with Cassie and all her problems but also with three bewildered children who couldn't understand why their father had left them. Dave had quite simply disappeared out of their lives. For a time he'd sent regular amounts of money but around a year ago even that had stopped and Cassie had had a letter from him saying that he had lost his job.

They had had a serious struggle to make ends meet. Cassie was in no fit state to work and Lara had only been working part time at St Joseph's in order to be able to help more at home. This, she knew, would have to change, especially now that Callum was at school full time, and if she'd been in any doubt, her resolve had been further reinforced by the steady arrival of yet more bills. They were sitting there now on the mantelpiece, staring her in the face—the familiar brown envelopes—and Lara knew there was no way they were simply going to go away.

She wasn't used to being short of money—in the

past she had worked full time on A and E and had been well on the way to a sister's position and a salary to match, but after Cassie's accident she had become very interested in the treatment of burns and had applied for a job on the burns unit at St Joseph's. That had been fine, financially, until Dave had left and Lara had taken the decision to move in with her sister. She'd given up her flat and had very quickly reached the conclusion that she would be unable to go on working full time. But that had been then. Things had changed now and she recognised that she needed to get back to full-time employment again. She would talk to Sue in the morning. Having made the decision, she felt better, and decided she would go and tell Cassie there and then.

After climbing the stairs and reaching the landing, through a half-open door she saw her sister in the bedroom she shared with Sophie. She was sitting on the bed and her shoulders were slumped.

'Cassie,' Lara said, tapping the door, 'can I come in?' When Cassie looked up Lara went straight in. 'Are you all right?' she asked anxiously as she saw the sign of tears on her sister's cheeks.

'It's all a mess, isn't it?' said Cassie, wiping her eyes.

'What is?' said Lara, sitting on the bed beside her and slipping one arm around her shoulders.

'Everything—money, the children, you, me…'

'Whoa, there, take it easy,' said Lara. 'Let's take this slowly, one thing at a time. The children are fine.'

'They're missing Dave,' said Cassie with a sniff.

'Yes, I know, but there's not a lot that we can do about that at the moment. Maybe when he gets another job he'll get in touch again. As for you, well, honestly, Cass, you are so much better, everyone can see it, you're doing so much more now. Which brings me on to money and what I'd come up to tell you.'

'The bills are mounting up again, Lara.'

'True,' Lara agreed, 'that's why I've decided to go back to full-time work again.'

'Really?' Cassie's eyes widened.

'Yes.' Lara nodded. 'Now that Callum's at school all day, I don't need to be here so much. I'm sure you can cope with meeting Callum from school, and the other two can come home on the school bus.'

'Well, yes, but—'

'We need the extra money, Cass.'

'Yes, I know, but, oh, Lara, it's all down to you again. It really isn't fair. We've taken over your life. You have no life of your own, you've lost your home—you haven't even got a decent sized bedroom—and you've lost your boyfriend…'

'That wasn't going anywhere,' said Lara quickly.

'But it might have done if we hadn't messed it all up for you.'

'Listen, Cassie.' Lara took her sister's hands. 'No one forced me to do what I did. I did it of my own free will because you and the kids were in trouble. You are my sister and they are my nephews and niece, and I love you all.'

'Oh, Lara.' Cassie's voice broke and the tears coursed freely down her cheeks and over the scars. 'I don't know what we would have done without you…'

'Things will get better, I promise you,' said Lara firmly. 'I'll get more hours and we'll settle those bills first, then we'll see what other improvements we can make to our lifestyle. As for men, who needs them?'

'You'll find someone else one day,' said Cassie, wiping her eyes with a tissue. 'I'm not sure that I want anyone else—after all, I have three children and I doubt anyone would look at me looking like this. But you…well, you're young and lovely, Lara, and you have your whole future before you. Someone will come along, you'll see.'

'I doubt it,' said Lara lightly. 'I never get to meet anyone.'

'You did today,' said Cassie.

'Today?' Lara frowned.

'Yes, your new Argentinean surgeon.'

'Oh, him,' she replied flippantly. 'He's hardly boyfriend material.'

'Pity,' said Cassie. 'I thought he sounded rather dishy.' She paused. 'Was he?' she added. 'Dishy, I mean?'

'Don't know, really.' Lara wrinkled her nose. 'He wasn't my type. Very dark, his hair so closely cropped I thought he was bald, tall, and I would imagine fantastically wealthy, as when he isn't working at St Joseph's he's operating on rich, spoilt women who want face lifts and tummy tucks.'

'Sounds rather interesting,' mused Cassie.

'Like I said, definitely not my type.'

'Just because the last man in your life was a Scandinavian, blond, outdoor type, it doesn't mean that anyone different has to be ruled out,' said Cassie mildly.

'I know that,' protested Lara, 'but the chemistry has to be there in the first place, doesn't it? Otherwise there's no attraction, and without that, well, there's no point, is there?'

'And there wasn't any spark with this guy—not even when you stopped and gave him a lift home?' asked Cassie innocently.

'No, of course not,' Lara retorted. 'I only gave him a lift because it was raining…and because…because I'd nearly killed him earlier, and I guess I may have been feeling a bit guilty about that.'

'I see,' said Cassie.

It was ridiculous, Lara thought as she made her way to the small, single room which had been hers since she'd moved in with Cassie and the children—one double being occupied by Cassie and her daughter and the other by the boys. Of course she hadn't been attracted to the new locum surgeon. As she had painstakingly explained to Katie and her sister, he quite definitely wasn't her type.

On the other hand, she had to admit, she had actually been very aware of him when he had sat beside her in her car—not, she supposed, that she could have been anything else given the size of the man and the close proximity necessitated by her little car. But, no, this had been something else, something fleeting, elusive even that she was unable to put her finger on. But attraction? No, surely not that, which, when she thought about it was just as well, given that Andres Ricardo quite obviously was as far removed from her world and lifestyle as it was possible to get.

Her previous boyfriend, the one Cassie had referred to, had indeed been very different. For a start he had been Swedish—a doctor on an exchange visit to the hospital where Lara had been working at the time. His name was Sven, and he'd been very blond with blue eyes and a toned, athletic body, no doubt as a result of all the sport he played. Lara had thought she had been in love with him at the time and he had certainly told her he loved her—frequently—but after she'd moved in with Cassie and she hadn't been able to see him so often, he'd changed and she'd found herself doubting his protestations of love. In the end they'd simply drifted apart. She'd heard that he'd been seen with someone else—that had hurt—but in time she'd got over him and by the time she'd been told that he'd returned to Sweden she really couldn't have cared less.

There had been no one since, there had quite literally not been the time. But when Lara thought about it she had to admit that it hadn't really bothered her, and in spite of Cassie's assertion that she had put her whole life on hold, she really didn't see it that way. Her sister had needed her and she had been there for her—it was as simple as that. They had always been close, even though Cassie was six years older, and when they had been children it had always been Cassie who had looked after Lara. Now the tables had turned and it was Lara's turn to care for Cassie. The last two years had been tough, she couldn't deny that, but she didn't regret her actions one little bit. And now it looked as if things might be about to change again.

While Lara had been talking to Cassie about their future, Andres had stepped off the train at Waterloo and taken a cab to Knightsbridge, to the quiet, tree-lined square and the elegant town house, which belonged to his mother and which, while he was in London, was his home. It was a tall, imposing building set on three floors and built in red brick in balanced, symmetrical Georgian style, with high sash windows and a central front door at the top of a short flight of stone steps. After paying the cab driver, he let himself into the house, the silence rushing out to meet him as he opened the door. He deactivated the alarm system and crossed the spacious tiled hallway to enter his study, where he found that his housekeeper had left the day's mail on the large mahogany desk. He was just flicking through the envelopes when the telephone on the desk rang.

'Andres?'

'Hello,' he replied, recognising the voice of his partner Theo. Cradling the receiver between his shoulder and chin, he began opening his mail.

'How did it go today?' asked Theo.

'Not so bad. In fact, pretty good really. It's a modern unit and the staff seem OK.'

'That's good—you weren't too sure about it, were you?'

'Still not, if the truth be known,' Andres replied. 'But, no doubt, time will tell. How were things with you today?'

'They were going all right,' Theo replied, 'until Belinda handed in her notice.'

'Belinda!' Andres shifted the phone to his other hand. 'Why did she do that?'

'Said she wants to spend more time with her family...but who knows? Anyway, it's left us in the lurch a bit.'

'What about the agency?'

'Well, we'll get on to them in the morning, then I'll guess we'll have to start interviewing again. I have to say, I thought we were done with all that for the time being.'

'I know,' Andres agreed, 'so did I, but I suppose it can't be helped and we'll only have to find a part-timer to cover Belinda's hours. I bet Arun wasn't too happy.'

'You can say that again. You know how he hates change of any kind. I keep telling him he's getting old.' Theo gave a short laugh. 'But, listen, while I think of it, Annabel says to tell you that we are having a dinner party on the fourteenth of next month.'

Andres's heart sank.

'She said to tell you now in plenty of time before you get booked up with anything else.'

'Right. OK. Thank her for me, won't you?'

'Yes, of course. See you tomorrow.'

'Yes, see you. Bye.'

Andres hung up and stared at the phone for a long moment then, after glancing at his desk calendar, he gave a groan. The fourteenth of February—Valentine's Day. He knew exactly what that would mean. Annabel would, no doubt, even now be lining up one of her friends to partner him at her dinner party—she'd done it before, not once but several times, and each time it had been something of a disaster because the girl in question had been as far removed from his ideal as was possible. He didn't know how to tell Annabel not to bother, that he quite simply wasn't interested, because he knew that by doing so he would offend her. She meant well, he knew that, and really he was rather fond of her and Theo. If only they would stop matchmaking and thinking they knew what was best for him. The last girl they had tried to pair him off with hadn't seemed to have a single thought in her head and had giggled incessantly throughout the meal—he shuddered at the memory. He had compared the unfortunate girl with Consuela, as he always did, and had, as always, found her wanting.

He and Consuela had been so right for each other. She had been his best friend, his wife, his lover and his soul mate, and he seriously doubted he would ever find anyone ever again to fulfil all those needs. He had attempted a couple of relationships in the last couple of years but in each case he had recognised that he had merely been using the woman and that when lust had spent its course, as with Annabel's friends, there had been nothing there. Sometimes he wondered if he was destined to spend the rest of his life alone, a prospect that, in his present frame of mind, seemed quite appealing.

Wandering out of his study, he climbed the wide staircase. Once in the large master bedroom with its dark oak furniture and burgundy and cream furnishings he rapidly undressed before stepping into the shower, letting the hot water course over his head and shoulders and down the length of his body, washing away the grime of London and the stresses and strains of the day.

Afterwards he dressed in jeans and a tracksuit top before sending out for a take-away meal. While he was waiting for it to arrive, he relaxed on the huge cream sofa in the sitting room, which overlooked the street, and flicked on the television. Aimlessly he hopped from channel to channel, not really finding anything he wanted to watch. Then, just as he was about to switch to the news channel, he stopped and stared at the screen. There was a film showing, something filmed in Australia, but it was the actress who was playing the lead who had caught his eye. There was something about her, with her flaming red hair and creamy complexion, that touched a chord somewhere deep inside him, even stirring the first strains of desire, something rare these days. And also strange when he thought about it, for red-haired women had never really attracted him before. So why this one, why now?

He leaned forward as the camera went in for a close-up, then his breath caught in his throat as the woman's mesmerising green eyes seemed to look straight into his. Red hair, creamy skin, green eyes. What was this—what did this remind him of? Then he remembered. The nurse, Lara? Was that her name? Yes, Lara, that was it—the one who had nearly run him over, the one who had given him a lift to the station. This woman, this actress reminded him of Lara. He stared at the screen, watching her carefully, aware with every turn of her head of a slight but growing sense of arousal. Then, to his dismay, the credits started to roll and the film was over.

'Damn,' he muttered under his breath. He flicked the off switch, sat back on the sofa and stared at the blank screen.

# CHAPTER THREE

'I PROMISE I'll be as gentle as I can.' Lara bent over the patient and prepared to remove the dressing that covered a large area on his chest and extended up and across his neck.

'It's gonna hurt...I know it's gonna hurt.' The patient, a young man called Michael Rowe, screwed up his face as Lara grasped one corner of the gauze dressing with tweezers and lifted it slowly and gently, a millimetre at a time. Michael had been brought to the unit a week previously after suffering severe burns in a house fire at his neighbour's home. He had sustained his injuries when he had forced his way into the house through dense smoke and flames and had rescued the neighbour's children from the blaze. His family and the local community were hailing him as a hero.

'That's looking good,' Lara said, as she removed the last section of dressing. 'No signs of infection and there's evidence of some healthy new blood vessels.'

'Sister Jackman said the surgeon will be coming to see me this morning,' said Michael as he exhaled and relaxed slightly.

'He'll certainly want to see these burns before he decides on any skin grafts,' Lara replied, 'so what I propose doing is to cover the wounds with just a light dressing until he arrives.'

She glanced up as a young woman wearing a white coat arrived at Michael's bedside. 'Ah,' she said, 'here's Lindy, our nutritionist, come to talk about your calorie intake.' With a smile at Lindy, she added, 'He's all yours, but be gentle with him. He's just had his dressings removed and he's a bit fragile at the moment.' Gathering up the soiled dressings and depositing them in a plastic bag for incineration, Lara wheeled the dressings trolley out of the bay and into one of the unit's sluice rooms, where she put the instruments she had used ready for sterilisation then set about disinfecting the trolley. As she worked she heard Sue's voice outside at the nurses' station. Sue had been off duty for the past two days so Lara hadn't had an opportunity to ask her about more hours. When she had finished her disinfecting she carefully washed and dried her hands then, on walking out of the sluice, found that Sue was at the desk and appeared to be alone.

'Sue,' she said, 'may I have a quick word?'

Sue looked up, frowned slightly then threw a glance in the direction of her office, the door of which was slightly open.

'It's all right,' said Lara quickly, imagining that Sue thought she wanted a private lengthy talk. 'It won't take a moment, and it isn't anything particularly private.'

'All right,' said Sue with a nod, 'what's the problem?'

'It's not really a problem,' Lara replied, 'although I guess it could become one in time. You see, Sue, I need more hours. I knew the day would come when I would need to go full time again and I think that time is now. Callum is at school now and, well, quite frankly we need the money…' She paused as she suddenly caught sight of Sue's expression. 'What is it?'

'Oh, Lara,' said Sue, 'if only you'd said something before. I've just taken on another part-timer—I really didn't think you'd be ready yet… Oh, I wish I'd known. I'm so sorry.'

'And there's nothing else?' asked Lara in dismay.

'Not at the moment there isn't, I'm afraid, but there might be in time. You know how often staff come and go.'

'I really need something now,' said Lara slowly, as in her mind's eye she saw the ever-growing pile of brown envelopes on the kitchen mantelpiece.

'Maybe you could get something in another department,' said Sue hopefully. 'I know A and E were looking for more staff just recently.'

'Yes.' Lara nodded. 'Maybe I can…' She looked up sharply as the door of Sue's office opened fully and Andres suddenly appeared. For some inexplicable reason her heart jumped at the sudden and unexpected sight of him. She hadn't seen him since he'd got out of her car on his first day on the unit. No doubt since then he'd been operating in his London clinic.

'Thank you, Sister.' He nodded at Sue, and Lara imagined he must have been using her office for going through the day's cases or maybe even for something as simple as using her phone. 'Good morning, Lara,' he added, to her amazement.

'Good morning, Mr Ricardo,' she murmured in reply. She might have called him Andres if Sue hadn't been there, but somehow she didn't quite dare, even though he had told her his first name as if he expected her to use it.

'Is Mr Rowe ready for me to see?' he asked, the question directed at Lara.

'Yes,' she replied, suddenly uncomfortably aware of Sue's expression, as if she was trying to fathom this unexpected familiarity between the locum surgeon and her staff nurse, a familiarity which certainly hadn't been present on the previous occasion they had met, when they had appeared to be at each other's throats. 'I've just changed his dressings,' she added.

'How are the wounds looking?' he asked, and still he looked at her rather than at Sue.

'Very good. There are definite signs of granulation, no infection and his blood pressure and heart rate are good.'

'So we could be looking at an autograft tomorrow?'

'Yes, possibly,' Lara replied, 'but you would need to see him first.'

'Of course. I suggest we go now.'

'Very well.' Lara glanced hesitantly at Sue who simply raised her eyebrows in a resigned fashion.

'You'd better take Mr Ricardo to see Michael,' she said.

Lara led the way onto the ward where they found Michael still talking to the nutritionist. They both looked up as Lara and the surgeon approached, then Lindy murmured an excuse and hurried away.

'Mr Rowe, it's nice to see you back with us,' said Andres. 'The last time I saw you, you weren't really aware of anything very much.'

'I know,' Michael replied. 'They tell me I was out of it for about three days. That was probably a good thing—at least I didn't have so much pain.'

'I sometimes think nature has a very good way of arranging these things,' said Andres. As he spoke he took Michael's chart from the end of his bed and began studying the readings.

'Will you be doing the skin grafts?' asked Michael.

'Not today,' Andres replied. 'Maybe tomorrow. But I'd like to have a look at your burns before I decide.'

Lara moved forward and for the second time that morning lifted the light gauze dressings covering Michael's wounds.

'Has anyone explained to you what might be possible in the way of skin grafts?' asked Andres, after he had carefully examined the wounds.

'The doctor came to see me yesterday,' Michael replied, 'and he said something about taking some skin from my thigh and using it on my neck, and maybe some for my hands.'

'That's right,' Andres agreed. 'That is exactly what I hope to do.'

Lara watched as with his fine, strong, surgeon's hands Andres gently touched the skin around the wounds on Michael's neck and on his hands, then equally gently examined the skin of the man's thighs on the proposed donor site.

'This is looking good,' he said at last, straightening up. 'Now, do you have any questions?'

'This part where you'll be taking the skin from...' Michael indicated his thighs. 'Will that hurt much afterwards?'

'It will be sore for some days,' Andres replied truthfully, 'but we will be able to give you something to help control the pain.' He paused and glanced up at Lara, then back at Michael again. 'I understand you saved the lives of two children,' he said.

'Yeah, well.' Michael looked embarrassed. 'Anyone would have done the same. I never had time to think about it—I just did it.'

'Nevertheless, it was very brave of you. Now, I want you to rest today and tomorrow I will see you in Theatre.'

He and Lara moved away from Michael's bed. 'I

understand you have someone else for me to see,' said Andres.

'Yes.' Lara nodded. 'A man was brought onto the unit in the night. He had been on night shift at the factory where he works and he was involved in an accident with chemicals. He received serious acid burns to his hands and on his face where some of the acid splashed. He was stabilised in A and E then brought to us.'

'I'll see him now,' said Andres.

The patient, Amtul Karinski, was only semi-conscious and was receiving fluids through an IV infusion, together with analgesics for pain relief. Katie was tending him and gently lifted his dressings so that Andres could examine the injuries.

'The burns are very deep,' said Andres. 'This often happens with acid burns—I have seen them reach the bone. These will require full-thickness skin grafting. I will see him again tomorrow and if he is conscious I will talk to him about possible donor sites.'

There were two other patients on the ward for Andres to see, and Lara found herself accompanying him. Usually this would have been Sue's job, but she seemed to have been delayed so, rather than waste the consultant's time, Lara simply carried on with the ward round. When it was over they returned to the nurses' station where Andres thanked her before disappearing down the corridor to his consulting room. As he did so Sue came out of her office and stared at Andres's retreating back before turning her attention to Lara.

'So what was all that about?' she asked.

'I'm sorry, Sue,' Lara said quickly. 'You appeared to be busy so I completed the round for you.'

'I wasn't meaning that,' Sue replied crisply. 'What

I meant was this new friendliness between you and Mr Ricardo. The last time he was here you could hardly seem to bear the sight of each other, and now—well!'

For some reason Lara felt the colour touch her cheeks as out of the corner of her eye she saw Katie approach the desk, her manner one of curiosity as if she sensed some sort of tension between Lara and the sister. 'Did I hear him call you Lara?' Sue went on relentlessly.

'What's all this?' Katie stared from one to the other.

'Lara here and our new consultant,' said Sue. 'They were at daggers drawn the other day if I'm not very much mistaken.'

'That's right,' Katie chipped in, more agog than ever now. 'That was after Lara had nearly mown him down. So what's changed?'

'It sounded very much to me as if they are now on first-name terms,' remarked Sue dryly.

'Really?' Katie swung round on her friend. 'So how did all this happen?'

'It's nothing to get excited about,' protested Lara. She was beginning to feel decidedly uncomfortable now. Sue never made any secret of the fact that she disliked over-familiarity between staff on her ward, and especially between her staff and consultant surgeons. 'It was the other day,' she said, and went on to explain what had happened when she had left the hospital.

Katie's eyes widened and Sue frowned. 'Did he accept your offer of a lift?' she asked, a little frostily, Lara thought. 'Was he happy to trust your driving, in spite of the fact that he'd accused you of speeding?'

'Obviously, yes,' Lara agreed. She was beginning to get a bit rattled now by Sue's manner. 'In fact,' she went on, 'he as good as apologised and admitted that he may not have been paying as much attention as he should.'

'What did you say to that?' Katie was obviously enjoying this.

'Well, to be honest, I ended up admitting that I just might have been going faster than I should.'

'Told you so, didn't I?' said Katie with a laugh.

'So you're saying all these mutual confessions led on to first-name terms?' asked Sue, raising one rather sceptical eyebrow.

'I don't really remember,' Lara replied, wrinkling her nose. 'We talked about this and that and I guess I must have called him Mr Ricardo—anyway, when he got out of the car he told me his name was Andres and I told him my name. Really, that's all there was to it—it was no big deal,' she protested when the two women continued staring at her.

Sue gave a sniff and began collecting up a pile of folders on the desk. 'This won't do,' she said briskly. 'All this standing about, gossiping. We have work to do.' With that she disappeared into her office and shut the door firmly behind her.

'I reckon she fancies him,' said Katie with a wicked chuckle.

'Probably.' Lara gave a sigh. 'Honestly, what a lot of fuss about nothing.'

'It wouldn't be nothing if she really does fancy him,' observed Katie, 'and she thought he was eyeing you.'

'Well, he wasn't eyeing me as you so charmingly put it,' snapped Lara. 'I've told you exactly what happened and that's all there is to it. And, besides, even if he *was* eyeing me, there's absolutely no way I'd be interested. I don't have the time or the energy for dating these days.'

'Did he really ask you to call him by his first name?' asked Katie.

'No, he simply told me what his name is and I told him mine.'

'What else did you talk about?' Katie clearly hadn't finished.

'Not a lot really—there wasn't that much time,' Lara protested. 'Let's face it, it isn't far from here to the station. I did ask him if he was missing Argentina, and he said that he missed the sun. And I also asked him about his clinic in London.'

'And what did he have to say about that?'

'Not a lot,' Lara replied. 'It's a private clinic dealing mainly with cosmetic surgery and he's in partnership with two other consultants.'

'Is he married?' Katie began tidying the desk.

'I've no idea,' said Lara. 'I would imagine so—a man like that at the height of his career.'

'The best ones generally are,' said Katie with a sigh. Then, as if she had just remembered, she said, 'Sue said you were asking for more hours.'

'Yes, I was,' Lara agreed. 'I can do more now that Callum is at school full time, but there's nothing here—Sue's just taken on someone else. I wish I'd known about that. Still, never mind, I'll just have to look further afield, that's all. Anyway,' she added, 'I'd best get on otherwise I'll have Sue breathing down my neck again.'

By lunchtime Andres had made up his mind, but when he went to look for Lara he was told that she'd gone to the staff canteen for a sandwich. He found her sitting at a table by the window in a shaft of rare sunshine that streamed into the large room and highlighted her auburn hair making it shine like burnished copper.

'Lara?' he said, and she looked up, startled, her green eyes widening in surprise to find him there. Briefly he thought of the girl he'd seen in the film, the girl who had stirred his senses and reminded him of Lara. 'Do you mind if I join you for a moment?'

'No,' she said, 'no, of course not.' She appeared flustered, moving her carton of fruit juice and packet of sandwiches. 'Are you having anything?'

'No,' he said, 'I'm not eating. I just wanted to ask you something.'

'Oh?' She looked mystified and as he sat down opposite her he again caught the scent of that light floral fragrance she wore. There was something about her that intrigued him but he knew he would do well to curb that instinct. In fact, he wasn't at all sure that he was doing the right thing where she was concerned. She had children and, even though there was no evidence of a wedding ring on her slim white hand, that didn't necessarily mean she wasn't married. Not that it would make any difference if she wasn't, he sharply reminded himself, for she didn't interest him in that way and quite simply there was no room for a woman in his life. 'I'm afraid I overheard you talking earlier,' he said, when it was obvious she was waiting for him to continue.

'I'm sorry?' She frowned as if she had no idea what he was talking about.

'When you were talking to Sister Jackman. I was in her office, checking some records,' he explained. 'The door was open and I heard you asking her for more hours.'

'Oh, that. Yes, I did,' she agreed.

'And she told you that she'd taken on someone else and that there wasn't anything for you at the present time—is that right?'

'Yes, it is, unfortunately.' She nodded then took a sip of her fruit juice.

'So what will you do?'

'I'll have to start looking in another department,' she said. 'I really do need more hours, you see. My…my circumstances have changed recently and whereas before I was happy to work part time because it suited me, I now find that I need to go back to full-time work.'

'I think I may be able to help you,' he said slowly, watching her face as he spoke, looking for her reaction, seeing the puzzled curiosity that passed across her features. 'Remember I told you about the clinic in London where I am in a partnership?'

'Yes…' She nodded uncertainly.

'Well, one of our nurses has handed in her notice—she worked part time and I wondered if you might be interested in the job.'

For one moment her green eyes lit up then they clouded slightly. 'Would it coincide with my hours here?' she asked doubtfully.

'Well, as far as I know, it's mainly afternoons and some evenings.'

'And I work mornings here…'

'That's what I thought.' He paused. 'Would you be interested? I'm sure we could make sure that the hours fit in with your work here.'

'Well…yes,' she said, and for some reason he felt his spirits lift. 'I think I would be interested.'

'Even if it is dealing with rich women who are dissatisfied with their looks?'

'Even that,' she said with a wry smile.

'In that case I will arrange for you to come in to the Roseberry Clinic for an interview with myself and my partners—is that all right?'

'Yes,' she said faintly. 'Yes, of course. And thank you, Mr—'

'Andres,' he said.

'Yes...Andres.'

'You'll never guess what happened today.'

'No, what?' said Cassie as she poured the tea.

'I asked Sue Jackman for more hours,' Lara replied, as she nibbled the edge of a biscuit.

'Oh, Lara.' Cassie paused and stared at her. 'I'm so afraid you are going to take on too much...'

'But she didn't have anything for me,' Lara went on.

'Well, we'll just have to manage,' said Cassie, 'tighten our belts for a bit.'

'No, wait, you haven't heard it all yet.' Lara leaned back in her chair. 'Remember I told you about our locum consultant surgeon the other day?'

'The man from Argentina?' Cassie looked up. 'The one you nearly ran over?'

'That's the one.' Lara nodded as an image of Andres in his black coat and fedora flashed into her mind. 'Well, he overheard Sue telling me she didn't have more hours for me and he...well, he offered me a job.'

'A job? What sort of a job?'

'I told you about his clinic in London, didn't I?'

'The cosmetic surgery place? Yes, you did.'

'Well, that's where the job is,' Lara said slowly. 'He came and found me in the canteen at lunchtime, and asked me if I'd be interested. It's a nursing post apparently and he seemed to think it was mainly afternoon hours, which would fit in with my job at St Joseph's.'

'What did you say?' Cassie was still staring at her as if she couldn't quite believe what she was hearing.

'Well, I suppose I must have sounded interested because he said he would arrange an interview with himself and his partners, then before I left the hospital at the end of my shift he came back to me and said he'd phoned them and that they'd like me to go in tomorrow afternoon.'

'Doesn't waste any time, does he?' said Cassie faintly.

'No, I suppose not,' Lara agreed. 'On the other hand, I dare say they need to replace the nurse who is leaving pretty quickly.'

'Will that be your sort of thing?' Cassie wrinkled her nose as she passed a mug of tea across the table to Lara. 'Face lifts for film stars and liposuction for rich, bored housewives?'

Lara hesitated before answering. 'I wondered that,' she said at last. 'In fact, I even made a remark to that effect to Andres…Mr Ricardo,' she corrected herself.

'Is that his name—Andres?' asked Cassie quickly.

'Yes, it is.'

'Do you call him by his first name?'

'Oh, don't you start.' Lara rolled her eyes. 'I've had enough of that from Sue and Katie. He simply told me his name. Anyway, what were we saying?'

'About face lifts and liposuction,' said Cassie. As she spoke she lifted one hand and her fingers played across the scarring on her own face.

'Oh, yes. Well, when I made that remark he made it his business to defend his work, and explained that some of the operations he performed were for deeply psychological reasons…'

'And some of them aren't,' added Cassie with a sigh.

'Presumably not,' Lara agreed. 'I don't doubt that the vast amount of funding comes from those that aren't. But I can't argue with that, Cassie. If Sue had offered me a full-time job on the unit, I would have taken it. As it is, there doesn't look as if there will be anything there for some time, so I thought I may as well give this a try. If I'm offered the post tomorrow and I really don't like what I see, I will turn it down.'

At that moment Callum came into the kitchen and sat down at the table between his mother and aunt. 'What are you talking about?' he said, looking from one to the other.

'Auntie Lara might be taking a new job,' explained his mother as she moved the plate of biscuits closer to Callum.

'Won't she work at the hospital any more?' asked Callum, helping himself to a chocolate digestive biscuit.

'Yes,' Lara answered, 'I'll still work at the hospital in the mornings, and if I get the new job I'll work there some afternoons.'

'Won't you be able to meet me from school any more?' Callum looked worried and Lara hastened to reassure him.

'Mummy's going to meet you,' she said, glancing at her sister.

'Is that right?' Callum still looked anxious.

'Yes, darling.' It was Cassie's turn to reassure him. 'I shall walk to the school in the afternoons to meet you when you come out. And Luke and Sophie will come home on the bus.' She turned to Lara. 'I think there's a bus I can get if it's raining.'

'You might see Daddy,' said Callum, breaking into the conversation. Both women turned to look at him but he went on calmly eating his biscuit, wiping the crumbs from around his mouth with the back of his hand.

'What did you say?' said Cassie sharply.

'You might see Daddy,' Callum repeated.

'Yes, I thought that was what you said, but what did you mean?' Cassie persisted.

'I saw him,' said Callum. 'I saw him today at play-time and I saw him last week as well.'

Cassie seemed speechless for a moment so Lara intervened. 'Where was he, darling?' she said calmly.

'By the railings, looking in,' Callum replied.

'Why didn't you say anything before?' asked Lara gently.

'I didn't think you'd believe me.' Callum wriggled himself down from his chair. 'You didn't believe me before when I said I saw him outside the supermarket.'

'Did he speak to you?' said Lara with a quick glance in Cassie's direction.

'No.' Callum shook his head. 'He was too far away. Can I go and play now?'

'Yes, all right.' Cassie nodded in an absent-minded fashion and Callum ran out of the kitchen. A moment later they heard him clumping up the stairs.

Lara looked at Cassie. 'Do you think it was Dave?' she said.

'Who knows?' Cassie shrugged. 'I didn't believe Callum before because I thought it was just wishful thinking on his part because he missed his father so much, but…I don't know. He seemed pretty sure, didn't he?'

'How would you feel about it if Dave was back in the area again?' asked Lara slowly.

'Well, he was the one to break contact when he lost his job, but if he is back around here again then I guess we would have to work something out so that he could see the children.'

'Will they want to see him?' asked Lara, remembering the terrible traumas there had been when Dave had first left.

'Callum will, certainly,' Cassie replied, 'and maybe Sophie. But I don't know about Luke—there's still a lot of anger in Luke.'

'And what about you?' asked Lara gently.

'What *about* me?' demanded Cassie. Suddenly the scars on her face seemed to stand out more lividly than ever. 'If you mean would I want to see him then the answer is no. I never want to see him again. I can't help it—he left us when we were all at our most vulnerable and quite honestly, Lara, I don't think I can ever forgive him for that.'

Consuela! Andres awoke with a start. She was right there with him, beside him in the bed. She had come back to him. With a surge of passion and emotion he turned to her, ready to gather her up into his arms, only to find the space beside him was empty. With a low moan of anguish he collapsed back onto his pillows. It had been a dream like all the others, but this one had seemed even more real than most. He had seen her—her melting, tantalising smile, her mane of glossy black hair, her long, tanned limbs as she had danced away from him on a sunlit beach, always just out of his reach. He could even smell her perfume, that heady, exotic scent she always wore, and if he concentrated really hard he could feel the soft texture of her skin beneath his hands and hear her voice as she called his name when he made love to her. But she was no longer there. Consuela had gone and would never be coming back.

He lay for a while staring up at the ceiling, watching the patterns made by a streetlight outside and remembering how it had once been when Consuela had been alive and they had lived what must have seemed to many a charmed life among the rich young professionals in Buenos Aires. But that was over now and he was here in London at the start of what was supposed to be the building of a new life. Maybe his friends were right. Perhaps it was time to move on—if only someone could show him how.

Turning his head, he looked at the digital clock beside his bed and saw that it was three-thirty. Knowing he wouldn't go back to sleep straight away, he pressed the switch on the bedside lamp, threw back the covers, swung his legs to the floor and stood up. He always slept naked and, reaching for a towelling bath robe on a hook on the back of the door, he struggled into it then padded out of his bedroom and downstairs to the kitchen where he poured himself a glass of milk. Taking the glass to the window, he raised the blind and stood looking out at the dark shapes in the garden below. It was raining yet again and somehow the sight of rivulets of water on the window-panes depressed him even more, and he found himself wondering if the London weather would ever get much better.

As the thought crossed his mind he remembered that when he had voiced a similar concern to Lara, saying he missed the hot sun and blue skies of his homeland, her reply had been, 'We have blue skies too—just give it time.' As his thoughts turned to Lara he found himself hoping he had done the right thing in mentioning the job at the Roseberry and arranging for her to have an interview the following day. He had felt sorry for her when he had heard her ask for more hours and be told that there were none and once again had found himself wondering about her circumstances—the fact that she had spoken of children yet wore no wedding ring. Was she a single parent, struggling to raise a family? She had seemed pleased if not eager when he had mentioned the job to her. He only hoped she wouldn't find it too much—her job at St Joseph's, her family commitments and the travelling to and from this new position. If, of course, she got through the interview and satisfied not only himself but his two partners that she was the right person for the job.

At last he turned from the window and made his way back to his bedroom, his dreams of earlier banished now to the shadows. Even though before he switched out the bedside light he glanced, as he always did, at the framed photograph of Consuela by his bed, his last thoughts before sleep claimed him again were of Lara and the way her green eyes had shone when he'd told her of the job at the Roseberry.

# CHAPTER FOUR

LARA didn't really like the London Underground. It wasn't that she didn't recognise the necessity of its invaluable system of travelling around London, but the simple fact of being beneath ground, of that sinking feeling she experienced every time she stood on the escalator that carried her down into the very bowels of the earth, disturbed her.

She'd been the same as a child when her parents had taken her and Cassie to the caves at Cheddar Gorge. Cassie had loved it but all Lara had experienced had been panic while they'd been underground, and then tremendous relief when they had finally stepped out into the fresh air and the warmth of sunshine had touched her face again.

Perhaps, she thought now, sandwiched between an enormous woman with dozens of carrier bags and a youth in a hooded jacket who chewed gum incessantly and seemed to have a small radio glued to his ear, if she got this job there might be a bus she could catch to the Roseberry from the main line station at Waterloo and she would be able to avoid the Underground altogether. For one wild moment she had even considered the possibility of driving into town that day but had just as quickly dismissed the idea when she considered the problem of parking. She'd had to change at Embankment and take the Circle Line to Sloane Square, and as she waited for her station she found herself wondering for the umpteenth time if she was making a huge mistake in going for this interview.

It had been kind of Andres to consider her, knowing how desperate she was for more hours, but she still wasn't entirely certain that cosmetic surgery was the type of work she wanted to do, even though she had defended the situation to Cassie. On the other hand, they really did need the extra money, so maybe it was simply a case of waiting to see what the place was like and whether or not she actually got through the interview and was offered the job.

Moments later she had reached her stop and after a few minutes on the escalator—somehow so much more exhilarating going up than going down—she stepped out onto the street and the noise and bustle of the London traffic. It was a cold, blustery day but at least it wasn't raining, and there were even short bursts of sunshine as the winter clouds raced across a pale blue sky. Lara paused outside the station to get her bearings then instinctively tightened the belt of her white trench coat and lifted the collar against the wind before setting off to her left in the direction of the clinic.

She wasn't sure what she had been expecting, she only knew she was surprised when a little later she found the Roseberry Clinic. It was a modern building, and as she stared at it Lara realised that subconsciously she had been expecting something older. Cleverly designed to fit in with the neighbouring buildings, it nevertheless appeared to have been purpose-built with its mellow brickwork, huge rounded windows, glass-fronted entrance and immaculate surrounding gardens.

At last, taking a deep breath, Lara made her way up to the front entrance where she entered through a revolving glass door. The welcome warmth of the reception area hit her immediately and somehow the whole area, with its comfortable armchairs and low tables with smoked glass tops, its thick pile carpet, the paintings on the walls and the elegant staff behind the reception desk, was more reminiscent of a luxurious hotel foyer than a medical clinic.

'May I help you?' One of the two receptionists looked up as Lara approached the desk.

'I've come for an interview,' Lara replied. 'My name is Lara Gregory.'

'If you would like to take a seat for a moment,' the young woman replied, 'I will inform the board that you are here.'

That sounded ominous, Lara thought as she perched on the edge of one of the armchairs. Andres had said his two partners would want to interview her—this sounded as if there was to be a whole board of directors present. Attending interviews was by no means top of Lara's list of favourite things to do, and as she waited she felt her stomach begin to churn. Maybe they would take one look at her and decide there was no way she was suitable for such an establishment as this and tell her she could go. Then she could high-tail it back to the station—even the Underground was preferable to this.

'Lara Gregory?'

Lost in the turmoil of her thoughts, she hadn't seen a young woman approach her table. 'Oh.' She looked up sharply. 'Yes, that's right.'

'I'm Lucinda Scott-Denness,' the woman replied, 'the Roseberry's secretary. Would you like to come with me?'

'Yes, yes, of course.' Lara stood up and with her heart thumping followed the woman through a set of glass doors and down a corridor with a rich, ruby-red carpet underfoot. They passed several closed doors until the secretary stopped at a door, which bore a notice stating that it was the boardroom. The woman tapped on the door and when a voice from within bade them enter she opened it, indicating for Lara to follow her.

Lara was aware of a large, airy room with huge, south-facing windows and a long oak table running its length. Seated at the table were five people—afterwards she was to remember feeling relieved that there weren't more—three men and two women. Andres was there, of course, and just for one moment his gaze met and held hers. Somehow Lara found this comforting, and the fact that he was there and had acknowledged her did something to ease her tension.

'This is Lara Gregory.' Lucinda Scott-Denness ushered Lara to a chair and the three men rose to their feet while everyone present murmured a greeting.

'Ms Gregory, welcome to the Roseberry,' said one of the men, remaining on his feet when the others sat down. Lara noticed he was fairly tall with thick, curly brown hair and rather piercing blue eyes. 'My name is Theo McFarlane,' he went on. 'I'm chairman of the board. These are my partners and co-directors—Andres Ricardo, whom you know, and Arun Chopa.' He indicted an Asian man seated on his left.

Lara was pleased that Andres hadn't concealed the fact that he knew her, and was just digesting this fact when Theo McFarlane indicated one of the women seated at the table. 'This,' he said, 'is Elizabeth Grey, our matron, who is in charge of our nursing staff.' Lara only had time to register a woman in her fifties, her dark hair streaked with grey and rising from a widow's peak, her expression inscrutable, before Theo McFarlane carried on talking.

'And this…' he indicated the other woman at the table '…is Helen Poynter, our administration manager. Now, Ms Gregory, or may we call you Lara?' He raised his eyebrows and when Lara nodded he said, 'Yes? Thank you. Now, Lara, you come to us for this interview with the highest possible recommendation—that of one of our directors—so in those circumstances I feel we can dispense with many of the questions we would normally ask, those, for example, regarding background and motivation.'

He paused and Lara found herself feeling thankful that she wasn't going to be asked to explain her rather complicated domestic situation.

'We also imagine your qualifications and nursing skills are of the high standard we require,' he went on. 'Maybe, however…' he glanced at Lara then at the others around the table '…you could tell us a little about the work you do at St Joseph's.'

Taking a deep breath and suddenly very aware of Andres, who was sitting directly opposite her and who hadn't seemed to take his eyes off her since she'd entered the room, Lara began to outline the nature of the work that was carried out on the burns unit and the very satisfying and rewarding nature of the skin grafts that followed so many of these injuries.

'May I ask how you came to work on this burns unit?' asked Arun Chopa when she had finished.

'A member of my family was involved in a fire,' she replied quietly, then, aware of the little frisson of interest in the room, she went on, 'It was my sister, actually, and it was the treatment she received at the time and my constant visits to her on the unit that led me to apply for a job there. Previously, I had been working in Accident and Emergency at a hospital in Sussex.'

'So why the Roseberry?' It was Elizabeth Grey with her watchful eyes who asked the question, and even as Lara struggled to find the right answer, Andres came to her rescue.

'I think,' he said, 'it's safe to say that Lara's circumstances are such that she needs more hours. She applied to St Joseph's to extend her hours but there was nothing available. I had just heard that there was a vacancy here and with Lara's experience with skin grafts I thought she might be suitable to fill that vacancy.'

'And you think you will be able to combine the two?' asked Elizabeth Grey.

'I believe I could.' Lara nodded.

'Where do you live?' Arun frowned at her over the top of his glasses.

'In Surrey—Byfield, actually.' She paused. 'I understand the hours here would be late afternoon or evening shifts. I could easily accommodate those hours with the early shifts I work at St Joseph's.'

They asked several more questions, mainly about Lara's nursing qualifications, the different courses she had done in the past and where she had completed her training. Then Theo McFarlane asked her if she would mind waiting outside. Lucinda Scott-Denness escorted her back to the waiting area in Reception where one of the receptionists brought her a cup of tea in a delicate porcelain cup and two tiny macaroon biscuits. Lara smothered a smile as she compared this hospitality to the vending machine on St Joseph's burns unit, which had a mind of its own, sometimes producing tea when coffee was required and vice versa, and always in stout polystyrene cups.

As she sipped the delicious tea and nibbled the biscuits, she found herself watching the people who came and went in Reception. For the most part they were expensively dressed, leather, fake fur, cashmere and fine wool being much in evidence, likewise designer jewellery, handbags and items of luggage. Some gave their names at the desk and were then taken to a lift which whisked them away to an upper floor—no doubt to a private suite where they would await the surgery for which they would have paid a fortune. While she was sitting there Lara recognised a well-known star of a television soap opera in spite of the huge dark glasses the woman wore, and by the time Lucinda Scott-Denness returned for her she was convinced that she had stepped into another world.

'Lara, come and sit down,' said Theo as she entered the boardroom for a second time. 'We won't keep you waiting any longer,' he went on as she sat down. 'My colleagues and I have decided to offer you the position here. Before you reach your decision as to whether or not you will accept, perhaps you might like to look over the hospital and discuss salary and conditions with Mrs Poynter.'

'Thank you,' said Lara, suddenly overcome by the situation and the fact that the board had reached a decision so quickly. 'Thank you, yes, I would like that.'

Theo McFarlane glanced at Lucinda and Lara assumed he was about to ask the secretary if she would show her around. Before he could do so, however, Andres rose to his feet. 'Come on, Lara,' he said. 'As it was me who got you into this, the least I can do is be the one to show you around.'

For some reason she felt her pulse quicken then realised that subconsciously she had been hoping that

Andres would be the one to perform that particular task. Moments later she found herself beside him as they walked the length of the ruby-carpeted corridor, which she quickly discovered led to the main part of the hospital.

'First of all,' he said as they walked, 'congratulations on being offered the post.'

'I imagine I have you to thank for that.' She threw him a sidelong glance.

'It was by no means a foregone conclusion,' he replied, drawing his dark eyebrows together. 'There were two other applicants we had to consider.'

'Really?' For some reason the thought lifted her spirits.

'Oh, yes,' he replied. 'Elizabeth Grey had one candidate lined up and there was another who has been trying to secure a position here for a very long time, but in the end you were by far the most suitable candidate for the post in view of your work at St Joseph's.'

'Even though I think I might find the actual work very different?' she asked, glancing up at him as they reached a set of doors, which he pushed open, standing back for her to precede him.

'I'm not sure that you will,' he replied. 'As I told you before, the actual surgery is very similar to the skin grafts that are carried out on any burns' unit.' He paused as they reached another set of doors. 'Through here are our operating theatres,' he explained.

'How many do you have?'

'Three,' he replied. 'Some of our work is carried out on a day-surgery basis but many clients are admitted the day before surgery then discharged the following day. More involved procedures require a longer stay, of course.'

'Is it just the three of you who operate?' asked Lara as she peeped into one of the theatres where support staff were cleaning and disinfecting the table and equipment.

'We have one registrar who works with us,' Andres explained. 'We also have three doctors who work shifts so that one of them is here at any given time. We also have a full nursing and ancillary staff. Now, we'll take the lift and I'll take you up to the clients' suites.'

The suites, with their almost hotel-like facilities, were the last word in luxury and a further visit, this time to the kitchens with their first-class chefs, indicated to Lara that the cuisine also left little to be desired.

Lastly Andres took her to his office and showed her the lists of operations that the clinic carried out. They ranged from face improvements—classical face lifts, nose refinements and 'bat' ear corrections—to figure improvements—breast enhancements, liposuction and tummy tucks.

'You quite obviously have some very wealthy clients,' Lara remarked.

'Yes,' Andres admitted, 'we have. We also have some very high-profile and well-known clients, celebrities and the like, which, of course, requires a high degree of confidentiality on our part.'

'But that surely applies to any medical situation.'

'Of course,' he agreed. 'The difference being between, say, St Joseph's and the Roseberry is that at St Joseph's you don't have members of the press camping outside, having got wind that some famous film star has booked in for a face lift, whereas at the Roseberry it happens all the time.'

'I hadn't realised that,' Lara said slowly. Glancing

out of the window at the neat flower-beds already showing signs of spring bulbs pushing up through the dark earth, she added, 'Are the initial consultations done here as well?'

'No.' Andres shook his head. 'We have other premises for those and for the follow-up appointments after surgery.'

'And where are those premises?' asked Lara.

'In Harley Street.'

'I should have guessed,' she replied with a short laugh, but the irony seemed lost on Andres.

'What do you think, Lara?' he asked at last. 'Do you think this job might suit you?'

'It's very different to anything I've done before,' she replied slowly. When he would have said something, she added quickly, 'Oh, I know you say the actual work is similar to what I do at St Joseph's, and it well may be, but I've never worked in the private sector before.'

'So it will be something of a challenge?'

'Yes,' she agreed, 'I suppose so…'

'I would have thought you might be someone who enjoys a challenge.' He paused. 'Or am I mistaken?' The dark eyebrows rose, questioning, the eyes beneath like black, unfathomable pools. Slightly disconcerted, Lara found herself looking away avoiding that direct gaze.

'No,' she admitted at last when it became clear he was waiting for some sort of answer. 'You're quite right. I do like a challenge.'

'So you'll be taking on this particular challenge?' he asked softly.

She took a deep breath. 'Yes,' she said at last, 'I will.'

'Good,' he said in the same soft tone, and as Lara

allowed herself to meet his gaze again, he added, 'I'm glad about that.'

After that he took her to the administrator's office where Helen Poynter gave her forms to fill in and discussed the salary and the hours that needed to be covered at the clinic. She established that she would be starting work there the following weekend. When they left the office, Andres walked back to Reception with her.

'I'll see you tomorrow, Lara,' he said as he escorted her to the entrance. 'I'm operating at St Joseph's in the morning.'

'Ah, yes,' she replied. 'Michael Rowe's skin grafts.' She paused. 'Thank you, Andres,' she said at last, 'for everything.'

'I hope you will be able to cope with it all,' he said uncertainly, as she would have pushed open the door.

'Cope?' She paused and looked up at him, puzzled by his concern.

'Yes, all your commitments,' he replied.

'Don't worry, I've made other arrangements. The only thing I might not be able to cope with,' she added dryly, 'is the Underground.'

'The Underground?' He frowned.

'Yes.' She gave a short laugh. 'I hate it. I've always hated being underground ever since I was a child—pathetic, isn't it?'

'Not at all.' He shook his head.

'I shall have to see if there is a bus I can catch from Waterloo,' she said.

'You could bring your car,' he said thoughtfully. 'There would be a parking space reserved for you here at the Roseberry once you are a member of staff.'

'Maybe I will. I would have to leave early to combat the traffic…'

'As most of your shifts are late afternoon, early evening and weekends, you might not find that so much of a problem as you think. Even the evening shift shouldn't be too bad because the bulk of the traffic will be pouring out of London as you travel in.'

'I'll think about it,' she replied. 'It's certainly worth considering.'

'How did you get here today?'

'The train, then the Tube.' She pulled a face.

'In that case, you must allow me to take you home,' he said.

'Oh, no,' she said quickly, horrified that he might think that she had been angling for a lift with her remarks about hating the Tube. 'I couldn't possibly let you to do that.'

'Why not?' He shrugged. 'I have no engagements this evening—it's the least I can do, having got you into all this.' He laughed and Lara realised it was the first time she had seen him really laugh. It transformed his serious, brooding features, revealing perfect, very white teeth and bringing light to his dark eyes. 'I insist,' he added, his words leaving no room for argument.

She waited for him while he returned briefly to his office, appearing a few moments later in a tan-coloured, leather, three-quarter-length coat over his black, roll-necked sweater and dark, beautifully cut trousers. He followed her through the revolving glass doors then with one hand beneath her elbow escorted her to the clinic's car park. It was kind of him to offer to take her home and really, deep down, she appreciated it, especially as it meant she would not have to do further battle on the Tube, but as he activated a remote control and they approached his car—sleek, black and foreign—she felt a moment's panic as she wondered what on earth she would do when they reached home. Should she ask him in? Offer him refreshment before his drive back into London? At least, she presumed he would be returning to London, but she had no idea where he lived or for that matter anything else about him at all.

And if she did ask him in, what would Cassie make of him? Knowing Cassie, she would have him lined up as a prospective boyfriend for her—she'd already hinted as much—which, when Lara thought about it, could be really embarrassing. And what of the children—what comments would they make? Maybe it would be better if she didn't say anything about him coming indoors. With that thought uppermost in her mind she sank into the luxurious leather of the passenger seat and fastened her safety belt.

Andres wasn't sure why he had offered to take Lara home and he wasn't certain either why he had instigated her coming for the interview at the Roseberry. There was something about her that attracted him—he'd been forced to admit that fact to himself and he hadn't really liked it. Andres had always been a man who had prided himself on having total control, over himself, his life, his job and his intentions, and it had never been his intention to allow himself to become attracted to another woman. A fling maybe, but not the sort of attraction that could lead to commitment. This had appeared to come right out of the blue.

He'd noticed Lara because of the ridiculous incident outside the hospital that first day and she had seemed to take up a sizeable proportion of his thoughts ever since. He didn't welcome it, because any such attraction inevitably meant a loosening of his attachment to Consuela, a fading of memories and incidents from his past, which was the last thing he wanted to happen. Maybe he should never have offered Lara the interview, but he had felt sorry for her and it was too late now. His colleagues had been impressed, not just with her nursing qualifications and experience with treating burns and skin grafts but also with her personality.

'She's a stunner,' Theo had murmured to him when Lara had gone out of the room to await the verdict of the board. 'No wonder you wanted her here.'

'Aren't you forgetting something?' he'd replied coolly.

'What's that?' Theo had looked mystified.

'She has a family.'

'Married?'

'Presumably.'

'Well, no doubt we'll find out when she fills in her personnel forms,' Theo had replied.

His friend's comments had irritated him, just as his and Annabel's constant attempts at matchmaking irritated him.

Now as he drove onto the A3 with Lara beside him in her white trench coat, with her auburn hair tumbling onto her shoulders and that light, floral but bewitching fragrance she wore filling the car, he found himself thinking that he was glad she had a family, glad she was married. He'd always drawn the line at married women so, provided he remained true to his own convictions, she should pose no further problem. The attraction would die a natural death, he would be able to treat her purely as a colleague and life would get back to normal.

'What did you think of the Roseberry?' he asked at last.

She seemed to give a little start at his words, almost as if she had been miles away. He wondered briefly what she had been thinking, realising as he did so that he knew very little about her. 'I was very impressed,' she replied at last. 'It…it wasn't quite what I had been expecting, I have to say.'

'In what way?' He was suddenly intrigued to know what she meant.

'Well, for a start, I was expecting an old building—you know, perhaps an old hospital or a converted school or something like that. I was quite surprised to find such a modern establishment.'

'It was purpose-built,' he explained. 'It was very fortunate that planning permission was granted, but I believe the sensitive designs of the architect swung the project in the end.' He paused and threw her a sidelong glance. 'What did you think of the nursing side of things?'

'It seemed very efficient. I like the matron system and I must say I rather liked the nursing uniforms—that dark blue with the white frilly caps. I can't remember the last time I wore a cap—it was years ago. And now, as you know, we wear trousers and tunics on the burns unit instead of dresses.'

'I was afraid you wouldn't like the uniforms,' he admitted with a chuckle.

'Not at all,' she replied. 'I think, however, it might take me a while to get used the private health-care system—suites as opposed to wards and clients instead of patients, and the freedom of choice they have in everything from menus to television channels and unlimited visiting.'

'You'll soon get used to it.'

They were silent for a while, Andres concentrating on his driving. Suddenly, unexpectedly, the sun broke through the cloud and Lara turned her head. 'You see,' she said, 'I told you we have blue skies and sunshine sometimes.'

'You did,' he agreed.

'Maybe not quite of the intensity of your Argentinean sun but still very pleasant.'

'I am familiar with English summers,' he said. 'My mother is English and although I have lived primarily in Argentina I was sent over here to school.'

'Where was that?' she asked.

'Eton,' he replied, 'and then university at Oxford before returning to Buenos Aires to medical school.'

'I see…' She appeared to hesitate. 'So where are you living now?' she added at last.

'In Knightsbridge,' he said. 'My mother owns a property there and she is only too pleased for me to make use of it while I am in this country.'

'Yes, quite,' she replied faintly. 'That must also be very handy for the Roseberry.'

'Yes, it is.'

'Are you intending to stay in this country long?' she asked after a long pause.

'The initial agreement with my partners is for two years, with the option of extending that time at the end if I wish.' By this time they had come off the A3 and were approaching the small town of Byfield. 'You will have to direct me to where you live,' he said.

'You could drop me off here near the precinct if you

like.' Just for a moment he thought he detected a note of something like desperation in her voice.

'Why?' he said. 'Do you have shopping to do?'

'Not really.'

'In that case, I will take you home.'

'I just thought it might be easier for you—it's a bit of a rabbit warren of streets...'

'Just direct me,' he said, his tone putting paid to any further argument.

She directed him through a heavily populated residential area, finally indicating a house in a long terrace behind an avenue of trees. He managed to find a parking space and backed the car into it. She seemed nervous and he wondered if her husband was around, and may be the type of man who didn't take kindly to his wife being brought home by someone he didn't know. Her next words, however, seemed to put paid to that theory. 'Would you...would you like to come in for a cup of tea or something?' she asked.

'That's kind of you...that is, if it's convenient.' His first instinct was to refuse, but suddenly, in spite of his earlier resolve not to allow himself to become personally involved with this woman any more than was strictly necessary, he found he was curious about her, about where and how she lived and about her family.

'It might be in a bit of a state—the children, you know...' she said as she unfastened her seat belt.

'Don't worry about that,' he said. As he turned to open the car door, he added curiously, 'Who looks after them when you are at work?'

'My sister,' she replied.

Her sister. He was surprised. He had expected her to say her husband—then found himself wondering if his earlier assumption had been correct and that Lara was indeed a single mother.

He followed her up to a house with a brightly painted front door and brass knocker and waited while she fumbled in her bag for her keys then inserted one in the lock. As the door swung open a small boy appeared in the hall, a boy with Lara's pale skin and auburn curls.

'Guess what I did?' He rushed headlong to the door then stopped dead when he saw that Lara wasn't alone and hung back shyly, hands behind his back.

'Callum,' Lara said, taking her key out of the lock, 'this is Mr Ricardo—say hello.'

'Hello,' mumbled the boy.

'Hello, Callum.' Andres held out his hand and after a moment's hesitation the boy briefly took it then turned and scampered back down the hall.

'He's a bit shy with strangers,' said Lara, 'but only to start with. Once he knows you there's no stopping him, so you have been warned.'

'He looks very much like you,' he said, then realised that as he spoke Lara had shut the door behind them with a loud click and hadn't heard what he had said.

'Sorry?' she said, pulling her scarf from around her neck and shaking out the wild mass of her hair.

'I said he looks like you,' Andres repeated. 'Your little boy.'

'My little boy…?' For a moment she looked bewildered then she gave a short laugh of realisation. 'Oh, you mean Callum?'

'Yes…' He frowned.

'Callum isn't my son,' she said. 'I'm not married. Callum is my nephew.'

He stared at her, aware that something had shifted, changed, although for the moment he couldn't think for the life of him exactly what it was.

## CHAPTER FIVE

'LARA, he's absolutely gorgeous!' It was an hour later and Lara had just returned from the front door after seeing Andres drive away in his car. Cassie was seated on the sofa and in front of her on the coffee-table were the remains of the tea and cake they had offered to their visitor.

'That may well be,' Lara replied darkly, 'but there's no point in you getting any ideas in that direction.'

'I don't see why not.' Cassie paused then, as if it had just occurred to her, she said, 'He isn't married, is he?'

'I've no idea,' Lara replied.

'You mean you haven't asked him?' Cassie stared at her.

'Why in the world would I ask him something like that?' Lara demanded, as she began stacking the cups and saucers onto the tray—the *best* cups and saucers, no less.

'I thought perhaps it might have come out in conversation,' said Cassie. 'After all, he seemed to have found out all about you.'

'Only just,' said Lara with a grin.

'What do you mean, only just?' Cassie frowned, the expression making the scars on her face stand out even more than usual.

'He thought I was married and that the children were mine,' she explained with a chuckle.

'*All* of them?' Cassie's eyes rounded.

'Yep, all of them.'

Cassie continued to stare at her then, at last, she said, 'So let me get this straight—he organised a job for you at his clinic, then went to all the trouble of bringing you home, even though he was under the impression that you were married with three children?'

'Yes,' Lara agreed, 'that's about it.'

'Now, why would he go to all that trouble?'

'I think he just happens to be that sort of man,' Lara replied with a little shrug.

'Wow,' said Cassie softly. 'He sounds too good to be true.'

'Exactly,' said Lara, picking up the tray. 'Like I say, he's probably married, and even if he isn't, well, there's no point in you reading anything into this.'

'I don't see why not,' Cassie began, but Lara cut her short.

'He lives in a different world, Cass,' she said, looking down at her sister. 'He's a rich, successful surgeon with wealthy parents who have homes in Knightsbridge and in South America. He was educated at Eton and Oxford—'

'What was the clinic like?' Cassie interrupted, seemingly unimpressed by Lara's litany of Andres's background.

'Again, out of this world,' Lara replied. 'The patients are for the most part wealthy women film stars and the like who are prepared to spend any amount to change the way they look. The clinic itself is like some luxurious hotel. Each patient, or client as they call them, has their own suite with bedroom, shower room and sitting room complete with cable television and telephone. They have a sauna, Jacuzzi and gym on the premises and a whole range of alternative treatments available from massage to acupuncture and aromatherapy. The cuisine is out of this world…'

'Bit like St Joseph's, then,' said Cassie with a grin.

'Yes, exactly like St Joseph's,' Lara replied wryly. 'Why, they even have—'

'Did you see that car?'

Lara broke off as Luke suddenly flung back the sitting-room door and stood there on the threshold, his face flushed and wearing a look of disbelief.

'It was fantastic,' he breathed. 'An Italian job. I couldn't quite catch the model—will you find out for me, Lara?'

'I'll see what I can do,' said Lara with a short laugh, 'but right now I'm going to tackle that pile of ironing.'

'I can do that,' said Cassie quickly.

'No, you won't,' Lara replied over her shoulder. 'You look exhausted. I'll do it.' Leaving Luke with his mother, she made her way to the kitchen, smiling as she did so at Cassie's reaction to Andres. Fancy her thinking that the surgeon could ever be interested in her, Lara. Why, even if he wasn't married, which seemed highly unlikely with his wealth, status and looks, he could probably have his pick of London's socialites. Cassie meant well, bless her, Lara thought as she stacked the dishwasher then set about the ironing, and she knew that her sister felt guilty that she, Lara, appeared to be wasting her life in devoting so much time to her and her children, but really Lara couldn't see what else she could do. Cassie was much better now but she still suffered from bouts of depression and Lara doubted she could cope with the children on her own for very long.

She smiled again as she recalled the expression on

Andres's face when he'd realised that Callum wasn't her son.

'So you live here with your sister and her children?' he'd said curiously as she'd shown him into the sitting room.

'Yes,' she'd explained. 'My sister was badly injured in a fire—'

'Ah, yes,' he'd said. 'I remember—this was the reason you became involved on the burns unit?'

'Yes, it was. Some while after the accident,' she'd continued when it had become apparent that he had been waiting for further explanation, 'my sister's marriage broke up and she wasn't able to cope, so I moved in here with her and went part time at St Joseph's in order to help her and the children.'

He'd stared at her, almost as if he hadn't been able to find words to express what he felt about this situation. In the end she'd come to his rescue by taking his coat, inviting him to sit down then leaving him for a moment in order to put the kettle on for tea. When she'd returned she'd brought Cassie back with her and introduced her to Andres.

He'd met the children, too, briefly, when they'd come into the sitting room on their way to the corner shop to buy sweets. For once the two older children had seemed in awe, lost for words at the overwhelming presence in their sitting room of this tall man with his expressive dark eyes. Only Callum had really chatted, as if in some way he felt superior to the other two in having met this stranger first. Andres had asked him about the football shirt he was wearing and Callum had happily told him all about his favourite team.

And now he'd gone and Lara still found it amusing to think that he had thought she was married and that the children were hers. Once he'd got over his surprise at finding out the truth, she was certain there had been pleasure in those dark eyes. Not that she read anything into that, of course, because as she'd already said to Cassie he was bound to be married himself, and even if for some obscure reason he wasn't, there was no way there could ever be anything between them. Quite simply, he lived in a different world from the one she inhabited.

In spite of that, as she worked steadily through the huge pile of ironing Lara found herself looking forward to her new job at the Roseberry Clinic with a tingle of excitement, something she hadn't experienced for a very long time. How much this had to do with the job itself and how much with the fact that she would be working with Andres Ricardo she wasn't really sure.

Slowly, meticulously, Andres moved the piece of skin a millimetre at a time, easing it into position on the wound on Michael Rowe's neck. He and the anaesthetist, Max Gunther, had agreed on a general anaesthetic for this particular patient in view of the complexity of the grafts required. He glanced up at the anaesthetist, who nodded slightly in response, indicating that all was well with the patient's blood pressure.

'What fixative do you propose using?' asked Tom Martin, the doctor who was assisting in Theatre that day.

'I intend using a laser with a dye normally used in ophthalmic operations,' Andres replied, as with forceps he carefully repositioned the skin, which he had earlier removed from Michael's inner thigh.

'Have you had good results with that?' asked Tom as he leaned closer to the patient for a better look.

'Yes.' Andres nodded. 'I used it first when I was practising in Buenos Aires—we found there was much less risk of further scarring with this method. When the dye is illuminated with a green light, it forms a strong bond with the surrounding tissue. I use it all the time now in my London clinic.'

The atmosphere in Theatre was somehow uplifting with classical music—Andres's choice—playing throughout the morning's operating schedule. He had inherited his love of music from his mother, and he found that somehow it always set the right tone, even among some of the younger members of staff who probably would never have thought of playing classical music in any other circumstances but who appeared to work along quite happily to Puccini or Verdi.

Lara was scrub nurse that morning and Andres had found their eyes meeting over their masks at the moment he'd strode into the theatre. She'd lowered her eyes almost as quickly but there had been no denying that spark of familiarity, the type of familiarity that had come from him taking tea with her and her family the previous day. He had been amazed to learn that none of the children were hers and somehow even more amazed that she had never been married—not that that should make any difference to him, of course. He wanted no such involvement, with Lara or with anyone else, not now, or in the foreseeable future. But he had still been surprised, nevertheless, for he had assumed that a woman like Lara would be bound to have a man in her life.

What had also surprised him had been the degree of selflessness shown by Lara towards her sister and her family. There couldn't be too many young women who would be prepared to put their personal lives on hold in such a fashion—he admired her for it. Even as the thought crossed his mind he looked up and across the operating table to where Lara was arranging instruments on a trolley. Her eyes were downcast now, the thick lashes sweeping the creamy curve of her cheek while at the nape of her neck two stray tendrils of hair had escaped from the blue theatre cap she wore. It made her appear vulnerable, and for a fleeting moment Andres had to fight the sudden ridiculous urge to cross the room and touch that tender area of skin. Then the moment was gone as Tom began discussing the second of the three skin grafts they were performing on Michael Rowe, this time on his right hand.

They worked on steadily until at last the laser bonding was complete and the theatre sister began applying light dressings to the donor and recipient sites.

'Thank you, everybody.' Andres pulled off his mask and gloves then the red cap which he always wore when operating and which had become something of a personal trade mark. Glancing around at his team as the patient was wheeled away into Recovery, he turned to Lara, who had removed her mask and was clearing away the instruments used in the skin grafts. 'Tell me, Lara,' he said, lowering his voice so that only she could hear, 'who carried out your sister's skin grafts? Was it Mr Sylvester?'

'No.' She shook her head and her eyes clouded over. 'I wish it had been him, but he was apparently away on holiday at the time and the grafts were carried out by a locum.' She paused and looked up anxiously at him. 'Why do you ask?' she said. 'Don't you think a satisfactory job was done?'

'It's not really for me to query a fellow colleague's work,' he replied, 'but, yes, you're right—I do think a better job could have been made of it.' He hesitated. 'Is Cassie herself happy with the results?'

'Not really,' Lara replied. 'There are times when she is in despair. She suffers badly from depression and, of course, her marriage breaking up did nothing to restore her confidence.'

'When exactly did her husband leave her?' Andres frowned. Folding his arms, he leaned against the table as he watched Lara clear up.

'Some time after the accident,' Lara said. 'I can't remember exactly when but he just didn't seem to be able to cope with any of it.'

'It can't have been a picnic for her either,' Andres remarked dryly.

'No. Quite,' Lara agreed.

'What about the children—do they see their father?' he asked curiously.

'They did to start with, then he moved away—something to do with his job. He works in computers. He sent money for a time, then he lost his job and Cassie was forced to get help from the state. There was less and less communication from Dave—that's his name,' she added, 'until eventually it stopped altogether.'

'How did that affect the children?' he asked. By this time Lara had finished her clearing up and together they walked out of the theatre and began to make their way back to the wards.

'Badly,' she replied. 'Luke became very angry and withdrawn, Sophie would cry at night and Callum, well, he used to wet the bed. Recently he's started saying he's seen his father—in the shopping precinct to start with.'

'And had he?' Andres raised his eyebrows as he

pushed open the doors that led onto the nurses' station and stood back for her to precede him.

'We didn't think so at first,' Lara replied, 'but now he's saying that he's seen his father outside his school.'

'And do you think there's any truth in that?'

'Who knows?' Lara shrugged, but he noticed a worried frown playing across her features, reminding him just how involved she was with her sister's family. 'He did seem very certain.'

'And what about your sister?'

'She doesn't want to know,' Lara replied. 'She said she didn't think she would ever be able to forgive him for what he did.'

'Understandable, I suppose, under the circumstances,' he said. They reached the desk, where they found Sue sitting in front of a computer and the little dark-haired staff nurse, whose name escaped him, eyeing himself and Lara with undisguised interest.

'How did it go?' Sue looked from Lara to himself then glanced quickly back at Lara.

'Very well,' he replied. 'I hope that young man will be pleased with the results. Now, Sister, I would like to go and see Amtul Karinski, please.'

'Very well.' Sue rose to her feet.

'Is he conscious now?' asked Andres.

'Yes, he is.'

'Good. In that case, we will be able to discuss skin grafts with him.'

'What was all that about?' demanded Katie, as Andres and Sue made their way onto the ward.

'All what?' said Lara. She had been hoping to make a quick getaway, but from the look on Katie's face she very much doubted that was going to be possible.

'You and him—our man from Argentina—heads together, deep in conversation...'

'He was asking me about Cassie's accident,' Lara replied firmly.

'How did he know about that?' Katie's eyes widened.

'He saw for himself,' she said, wishing she hadn't got into this particular conversation.

'How? When?' Katie looked more puzzled than ever and Lara knew she would need to give her friend a pretty detailed account of all that had transpired in recent days.

'Actually, Kate, I've got quite a lot to tell you.' She glanced up at the clock above the nurses' station. 'How about we go for a break now?'

Ten minutes later the pair of them were in the staff canteen having a hasty sandwich and a coffee while Lara brought her friend up to date with what had been happening. She had just got to the part where Andres had taken her home and met Cassie and the children when Katie stopped her.

'Hang on a minute.' Katie leaned forward and looped her hair back behind her ears. 'Let me get this straight. You say he offered you a job at this fancy clinic of his, but how did he know you wanted a job in the first place? Did he not think you were happy here, or is he in the habit of poaching staff?'

'No, of course not. He happened to overhear me asking Sue for more hours and Sue telling me that she didn't have anything to offer me at the moment. As it happened, a nurse at the clinic had just handed in her notice, so he approached me and asked if I would be interested.'

'Just like that?' Katie's eyes widened.

'Yes, well, like I said,' Lara continued, 'I had to go for an interview in London at the Roseberry Clinic. It was a bit nerve-racking actually. The board of directors was there, and the matron, and the hospital administrator...'

'And then he took you home?'

'Well, yes.' She nodded. 'After they'd told me that the job was mine if I wanted it.'

'I would have said that was something of a foregone conclusion, wouldn't you?' Katie raised one eyebrow. 'What with you being sponsored by a member of the board, so to speak.'

'Not at all,' Lara replied hotly. 'Andres—Mr Ricardo,' she hastily checked herself, but not before she'd seen the smile that crossed Katie's features, 'told me that there had been two others in line for the job.'

'But they chose you.'

'Yes.' She paused then, goaded by something in Katie's attitude, she said, 'Why are you being like this, Katie? I thought you'd be pleased for me—you of all people know how difficult it's been for me, with Cassie and the children and everything.'

'I just don't want you getting hurt,' muttered Katie, taking a mouthful of her coffee.

'But why should I get hurt?' Lara stared at her friend in bewilderment. 'It's only a job we're talking about, for heaven's sake.'

'Yeah, right.'

'It *is*, Katie,' she emphasised. 'And if it doesn't work out, I shall pack it in—it's as simple as that.'

'Why did he take you home?' Katie clearly hadn't finished.

Lara sighed. 'I happened to say I wasn't keen on the Underground, and he offered to drive me home.'

'So what's going to happen in the future? Is he going to come and get you every day then bring you home again afterwards?'

'No, of course not.' Lara felt her cheeks flush and the beginnings of a headache over her right eye. 'I shall be working mainly afternoons and evenings and some weekends, so I propose driving in myself,' she said. Really, she didn't know why she was going to all these lengths to defend her position to Katie, friend or no friend, because it wasn't actually any of Katie's business what she did.

'Does Sue know about any of this yet?' asked Katie suddenly.

'No.'

'Oh, boy!' said Katie, pulling a face.

'Why?' Lara stared at her. 'What difference should it make to her? After all, I did ask her first for more hours—it was hardly my fault that she couldn't give me any.'

'Because she fancies him, that's why,' declared Katie, leaning back in her chair. 'I told you she did.'

'Yes, I know that's what you said,' said Lara slowly, 'but I didn't really think… I mean, let's face it, Katie, he's probably married so he wouldn't look twice at—'

'He isn't,' interrupted Katie flatly.

'Isn't what?' Lara frowned.

'He isn't married.'

'How do you know that?' Lara was suddenly aware of a prickling sensation at the back of her neck.

'He told Tom Martin,' Katie replied, 'and Tom told Sue.'

'So he's single…'

'Sort of,' said Katie. 'He's a widower actually. His wife died a few years ago—so our sainted Sister

Jackman thinks she's in with a chance. I can't imagine what she'll make of it when she knows that he's given you a job and that he's been careering about all over London with you, not to mention meeting your family.'

'It wasn't like that!'

'No?' Katie grinned. 'You try telling Sue that...and after all the trouble she's going to as well.'

'What trouble?' Lara narrowed her eyes.

'Didn't you notice the highlights this morning?'

'I've been in Theatre.' Lara frowned. 'What highlights?'

'Oh, the works,' said Katie calmly, as she peeled a banana and bit off the top. 'Top salon job, I would say. She's out to get him, Lara,' she added with a sudden chuckle, 'so don't say you haven't been warned.'

'This is getting ridiculous,' Lara protested. 'Andres Ricardo may have got me a job—for which I'm very grateful—but that is honestly as far as it goes. I'm not interested in him and I'm pretty darned certain he isn't interested in me.'

'So can you honestly say that if he was to ask you out, you would turn him down?' asked Katie calmly, as she finished her banana and placed the skin on her plate. When Lara didn't immediately reply, she leaned forward slightly so that she could look up into her face. 'Lara?' she probed.

'What?' In growing exasperation Lara looked at Katie.

'What I said,' Katie replied. 'If our highly fanciable new surgeon asked you out, would you go or would you turn him down?'

'He's hardly likely to ask me out,' protested Lara.

'Why not?' Katie's eyes narrowed. 'He's free apparently—and so are you, so there's no problem there.'

'Katie—we're chalk and cheese,' Lara began.

'How do you mean?'

'Well, his world is as far removed from mine as it's possible to be—he lives in Knightsbridge, for heaven's sake.'

'So?' Katie shrugged. 'You live in Byfield. What's the big deal?'

'He's a top surgeon.'

'And you're a staff nurse.'

'He's fantastically rich.'

'And you're skint. Can't see the problem myself.' Katie laughed and Lara found herself joining in. 'Let's face it,' Katie went on after a moment, 'Cinderella and her prince were poles apart, but look what happened to them. And if there is going to be a fairy-tale romance, I'd far rather it was between him and you than him and our sour-faced colleague who, incidentally, is old enough to be his mother.'

'Oh, Katie.' When Lara had finished laughing she shook her head. 'I know you mean well and I know you want something to happen in my life, but I really don't think you should hold your breath where Andres Ricardo is concerned.'

'But you still haven't answered my question,' Katie persisted.

'Which was?'

'If he asked you out, would you go?'

'But he wouldn't.'

'If he did.'

'Would *you*?'

'We weren't talking about me,' Katie retorted, 'but, since you ask, yes, too right I would. Like a shot. So…?'

'Well.' Lara shrugged. 'Yes, I suppose I would.'

'Yes!' Katie punched the air with her closed fist.

'But there's no point getting excited because it just isn't going to happen—not in a million years.'

'You never know...' Katie's voice took on a defensive note but Lara carried on talking, ignoring her friend's last remark.

'And I also think it's time we were getting back to work otherwise we could be in trouble and I could find myself looking for yet another job.'

'True,' Katie agreed. 'Speaking of which, I think you would do well to tell Sue about your new job before she hears it from anyone else.'

'Yes.' Lara sighed as she stood up. 'I guess you're right.'

Together they made their way back to the ward where Lara tried to put all thoughts of what had happened out of her mind and get on with the job in hand, but as her shift wore on she found it increasingly difficult to concentrate. Katie's words kept reverberating in her head, especially the part about Andres being a widower. She wasn't sure why that should concern her so much—the fact that he was free. Before, she had been able to dismiss insinuations from Katie or Cassie about any attraction between herself and the new locum by using as her defence the fact that he was bound to be married—a man of his appearance and status. Now that defence no longer applied. He was free, and so was she.

So was she attracted to him?

Reluctantly she was forced to admit that she was. Not, of course, that that should make the slightest bit of difference because there was absolutely no way that he would ever even notice her in that way, let alone ask her out.

While Lara had been talking to Katie, Andres and Sue were talking to Amtul Karinski about the skin grafts that Andres intended carrying out on his hands.

'I think in a couple of days' time,' Andres said gently to the man in the bed, who was obviously still shocked and traumatised by the extent of the injuries he had sustained from chemicals at the factory where he worked. 'What I propose is taking some skin from your leg and grafting it onto these badly burned areas on your hands and across the tops of your feet where the acid burnt away your shoes.'

'I able to work again?' The man looked agitated and his heavily accented voice wavered.

'Not immediately,' Andres replied, 'but hopefully in time.'

'I lose my work permit.'

'You mustn't worry about that now,' said Sue as she smoothed his covers.

'But my wife...my children...' Amtul was clearly working himself up into a state of anxiety.

'I think, Sister,' said Andres as they moved out of earshot, 'a sedative and maybe a visit from the hospital social worker?'

'Of course.' Sue nodded and made a note on her pad.

'Where is he from?' asked Andres as they began to walk back to the nurses' station.

'He's an immigrant from Eastern Europe,' Sue replied. 'Romania, I think. Apparently, there's been a huge outcry over the fact that the health and safety regulations hadn't been properly carried out at the chemical factory where he was working. Something to do with the language barrier, I believe.'

'Has his wife been to see him?' asked Andres.

'Oh, yes,' Sue replied. 'I had to ask her to go last night. She thought she could stay here all the time.'

'Maybe that could have been arranged,' murmured Andres, 'under the circumstances.'

'And the five children?' said Sue, raising one eyebrow.

'Oh,' he said, 'I see. I was merely thinking of how difficult it is for families when someone is involved in an accident like this. It's bad enough when it happens in one's own country, and even then it can have disastrous consequences.'

'That's what happened with Lara Gregory's sister. After her accident her husband left her because he couldn't cope with the situation. Lara moved in with her sister and has helped enormously, but I believe they still have many financial problems.'

'So I believe,' Andres replied. 'Well, let's hope that situation will now be eased somewhat,' he added.

'What do you mean?' Sue frowned.

'Now that Lara has some extra work.'

'I don't understand—what extra work?'

'At the clinic,' he said.

'Clinic? What clinic?' The frown on Sue's face deepened.

'My clinic—the Roseberry.' Andres was surprised that Sue didn't know. She appeared to him to be the sort of person who would know everything that was going on in her ward, and then it suddenly occurred to him that Lara might not have wanted her to know. 'I knew Lara needed more hours,' he went on in an attempt to ease the situation. 'I overheard you telling her there was nothing here so I offered her part-time work at the Roseberry.'

'I see.' Sue's tone was decidedly frosty.

'I trust there will be no conflict of interests.'

'I don't like my staff moonlighting,' Sue replied crisply.

'It's hardly that,' Andres said. 'After all, it's not as if she works full time here and would be going on to do extra work. Her hours at the Roseberry will be mainly late afternoons, evenings and weekends, and I understand the shifts she does here are all early shifts—isn't that so?'

'Well, yes,' Sue conceded, but Andres got the impression she was still annoyed, if not by his having offered Lara work then by Lara accepting it.

'I'm sure there won't be any problem,' he said smoothly, 'and if it's going to help the situation for Lara at home, it will all be worthwhile.'

'Yes, I suppose so.' Sue was forced to agree with him, albeit reluctantly.

'It may also help to boost Cassie's confidence if she has to go out more, meeting the children from school and that sort of thing.'

She stared up at him. 'You've met Cassie?' she said at last, and for a moment Andres could have sworn there was a touch of suspicion, even accusation, in her voice.

'Yes,' he replied. 'I met her when I gave Lara a lift home after her interview at the Roseberry.'

'I see. Right, well, there seems to have been an awful lot going on around here which I knew nothing about.' Sue took a deep breath. 'So, Mr Ricardo, is there anything else that I should know?'

'I don't think so, Sister,' Andres replied, 'so if you don't have anyone else for me to see, how about we adjourn to your office and you make me some coffee?'

'Oh, right, yes, of course.' Colour touched Sue's cheeks, and with a barely audible sigh of relief at the knowledge that he had hopefully smoothed things over for Lara, Andres followed Sue into her office.

# CHAPTER SIX

'LARA, there are three admissions for tomorrow's theatre list—I'd like you to take their medical and personal histories, please.'

'Of course, Sister. Do I do that in their rooms or do they come to a treatment room?' It was her first shift at the Roseberry and Lara was still rather bewildered by the procedures, some of which were very different from those at St Joseph's.

'You go to them.' Sister Jennings sounded a little shocked, as if the very idea of the clients being asked to go anywhere was totally alien. 'Now, here is the list and their suite numbers.' She handed Lara a clipboard. 'Oh, and, Lara, your hair is escaping from your cap.'

'Oh, no, not again.' Lara put one hand to her head and attempted to tuck stray curls into the white frilly cap. 'I'm not used to wearing a cap,' she said.

'You don't wear one at your other hospital?' Celia Jennings raised her eyebrows.

'No, we don't,' Lara replied. 'At least, only when we are in Theatre.'

'I think it's a shame all these niceties are being dropped.' Celia wrinkled her nose as if she had just encountered an unpleasant smell then proceeded on to her office, not giving Lara a chance to comment further.

With a little sigh Lara consulted the list she had been given and found that of the three clients, two were women and one a man. The check lists for medical and personal history were thankfully very similar to those she was familiar with, and another quick check revealed that all three patients, or clients as she was desperately trying to think of them, were in suites on the second floor. Still fiddling with truant strands of her hair, she took the lift and moments later stepped out into the calm, tranquil atmosphere of the landing that housed the majority of the Roseberry's clients.

After a further check of the room numbers she tapped on one door, which bore the number twenty-two. A female voice bade her enter and as she pushed open the door she saw a middle-aged woman seated on a stool in front of the dressing table, gazing anxiously into the mirror. 'Mrs Roberts?' asked Lara, and the woman half turned her head. 'Mrs Stephanie Roberts?'

'Yes, that's right.' The woman nodded.

'I'm Staff Nurse Lara Gregory, I've just come to take a few details from you.' Lara pulled out a chair as she spoke and, sitting down beside the woman, consulted the notes on the clipboard. 'I see you are scheduled for surgery tomorrow,' she went on. 'A full, classical face lift, and Mr Ricardo is your surgeon.'

'Yes.' The woman nodded again then gave a short laugh that had a rather bitter edge to it. 'I'm finally submitting to the knife,' she said. 'I've battled with the idea for a very long time and I've now just about plucked up enough courage to go ahead with it—that's if I don't escape and make a run for it during the night.'

'I'm sure you won't do that,' said Lara, trying to sound as reassuring as she could but finding it difficult to equate this woman's need for surgery with that of the burns victims she was used to treating. 'Now,' she went on, 'if we could just talk about your medical history. Have you had any operations in the past?'

'Yes, I had both my children by Caesarean section and five years ago I had my gall bladder removed.'

'Was this by keyhole surgery or the traditional method?'

'The traditional way—I have the scar to prove it.'

'And did you have any problems with the anaesthetic?' asked Lara, as she filled in the appropriate boxes on the forms.

'I was very sick afterwards.'

'We'll tell the anaesthetist that,' said Lara, making a note, 'then he will be able to take preventative measures so it won't happen again. Now, what about previous illnesses?'

'I have recurring bouts of bronchitis, usually in the winter—but that's about all. We…we used to winter in Spain to try to avoid my bronchitis, but…' She hesitated. 'That was before…that was some time ago. I love the sun and I know I have sun damage on my face, which probably hasn't helped.'

'And what about medication?' Lara glanced up. 'Are you taking anything at the moment?'

'Only supplements—you know, extra vitamins, that sort of thing. Oh, and the antidepressants, of course.'

'How long have you been taking those?'

A frown crossed Stephanie Roberts's features, throwing them into sharp relief. 'Well, since…' She trailed off. 'About two years.'

'That's all right.' Lara nodded. 'Now, just a few lifestyle questions, Mrs Roberts. First of all, do you smoke?'

'No.' She shook her head.

'Have you ever smoked?'

'Yes—I gave it up about five years ago.'

'And were you a heavy smoker?'

'About twenty a day.'

'And what about alcohol?' Lara glanced up again from her forms.

'What *about* alcohol!' Stephanie gave another, short, bitter laugh. 'I have to have something, you know—that's about all that's left.'

'Can you give me some idea how many units per week?'

'Not really.' She shrugged. 'I look forward to my G and T in the evenings, wine with dinner, sometimes at lunchtime. Like I say, I don't really know—I don't keep count.'

'So probably more than the recommended weekly guidelines?'

'Yes, probably.' Stephanie fell silent as Lara carried on filling in the forms.

'Who is your next of kin?' Lara asked, looking up at last.

'My daughter, I suppose—unless an ex-husband counts.'

'How old is your daughter?' asked Lara, her pen poised over the clipboard.

'Twenty-two.'

'She will do fine. I just need to put down a contact name really.'

'I lost my confidence,' said Stephanie after a moment, and when Lara looked up again she went on. 'When he left me, you know.'

'Your husband?'

'Yes.' She gulped and nodded. 'We'd been married twenty-five years and he left me for a girl barely older than our daughter. My confidence was shot to pieces…and it was only then that I realised how old I was looking…'

'Surely that wasn't your husband's reason?' murmured Lara.

'Oh, he didn't say that in so many words, but it's pretty obvious, isn't it? People have said that this girl he's with looks just like me when I was younger. Anyway, at last I've decided to do something about it. You see…' she straightened her shoulders and tossed back her hair '…soon I shall be a new woman, thanks to Mr Ricardo.'

When Lara had completed her forms she left Stephanie and went to the next suite, where she carried out the same procedure with Edward Millington, a young man who was to have surgery the following day to correct his protruding ears.

'I'm dreading it,' he confessed to Lara, after she had asked him all the routine questions about previous operations, illnesses and medication, 'but I'd really reached the stage where I couldn't stand it any more. I'm due to go up to university soon and the thought of all the jokes and taunts that I've had all my life starting all over again as I meet a whole new lot of people was more than I could cope with, so I decided to go for it this time.'

'Have you considered it before?' asked Lara.

'Oh, yes,' he replied. 'Many times. I've even reached this stage before but I could never go through with it—chickened out at the last moment. But this time I'm determined to see it through.'

'Good for you,' said Lara. 'I'm sure you won't regret it.'

The third patient for admission was a woman who was to have surgery for breast reduction. She told Lara she was tired of being a figure of fun and just wanted to be normal.

* * *

'I've been forced to change my opinion a bit where cosmetic surgery is concerned,' Lara told Cassie after that first shift at the Roseberry. 'Behind practically every desire for surgery there is a story of some sort of human suffering.'

'Even if it's only vanity?' asked Cassie.

'Even that,' Lara agreed. 'The aging actress who feels she is facing the end of her career because of the way she looks can be suffering inside just as deeply as the person who wants corrective surgery for, say, a prominent nose.'

'Did you see much of Andres?' Cassie asked curiously.

'No, not really.' Lara shook her head. 'He was in Theatre and from what I can gather, when he isn't operating he's more often than not at the Harley Street consulting rooms.' She didn't add that she'd been disappointed not to see him during that first shift, but just as she had been only too painfully aware that she had been looking for him, she had also been on edge, waiting for him to appear. In the end she'd had to be content with a brief glimpse of him in the theatre when she'd gone to Recovery to bring a client back to her room. He'd seen her, come to the door and said, 'Lara, how's it going?'

'Fine, thank you,' she'd replied. And that had been all. The doors had closed and she'd no longer been able to see him. And at the end of her shift she'd left the clinic and driven home through the damp February night, feeling strangely depressed. Why she should feel this way she had no idea. She had needed a job and Andres had given her that job. Really, that should be that. Maybe she should feel grateful, but that surely was all.

So if that was the case, why did she feel this way, a mixture of restlessness and depression? What had she been expecting to happen, for heaven's sake? Had she allowed her head to be turned by Cassie's and Katie's assumptions that there was more to the whole thing—that Andres had some sort of ulterior motive in offering her a job, that he was interested in her in some way? She had told them both that the very idea was ridiculous, that she and the surgeon were worlds apart, so why couldn't she believe that herself?

She didn't see him for the next few days at St Joseph's either because when it was her shift he was off duty or vice versa, and by the time she did see him again, which was towards the end of her second shift at the Roseberry, she had made a supreme effort to get her feelings under control and dismiss him from her thoughts. She would be civil to him if their paths crossed, but that was all.

'Lara,' he said, coming out of a room and encountering her unexpectedly in a corridor. One word. That was all, but it was all that was needed to melt her earlier resolve to be merely civil to him.

'Hello,' she said. She wasn't sure whether to call him Andres or Mr Ricardo. She was pretty certain that Sister Jennings would expect her to say Mr Ricardo when they were on duty, just as Sue Jackman would expect the same at St Joseph's—but they were alone in the corridor and somehow, instinctively, Lara knew what Andres himself would expect. 'Andres,' she added almost shyly.

'I've been wondering how you've been getting on,' he said, that rare smile lighting his face, 'but I haven't seen you anywhere. I asked at St Joseph's but they said you were off duty.'

'And when I was there you were off duty,' she added with a little laugh.

He glanced at his watch. 'What time do you finish this evening?' he asked.

'Eight o'clock,' she replied.

'Why don't we go somewhere for a quick drink before you go home?'

She was aware that her heart leapt but her head urged caution. 'Well, I don't know…' she began.

'Can't you phone Cassie and say you will be a little late?' he said, effectively destroying any excuse she might have been about to make.

'Yes, I suppose I can.'

'Good—I'll meet you in the foyer at eight o'clock.'

'Yes, all right.' She turned and walked away from him down the corridor, outwardly calm and serene but inwardly with her heart thumping with excitement.

She was a couple of minutes late, having been delayed with a client who'd wanted to talk, but true to his word Andres was there waiting for her in Reception. In his black overcoat he looked every inch the successful consultant surgeon, and Lara found herself thankful that she'd chosen to wear her white trench coat, polo-necked sweater, tailored trousers and her leather boots, in which she knew she looked good.

He was sitting at one of the tables, leafing through the pages of a magazine, but he looked up as she entered Reception, tossed the magazine aside and stood up.

'Sorry I'm late,' she said. 'A client, you know…'

He waved aside her apologies. 'Do you have your car?' he said, and when she nodded he went on, 'I suggest we leave it here. There's a little place just round the corner where we can go.'

Andres wasn't certain why he had asked Lara to go for a drink with him. He hadn't planned it but, when he had come across her unexpectedly in the corridor, a sudden impulse had urged him to do so. Whether the fact that he had been thinking about her had anything to do with it or not, he didn't really know. He only knew he had found himself uttering the words and feeling ridiculously pleased when she had accepted. And as for thinking about her—well, for some reason which he was at a loss to explain he had found her slipping into his thoughts at the most inopportune moments. When he was operating, his favourite opera would be playing, and at the most passionate part of the music she would be there in his mind. The picture he had of her was always the same—she would be alone, wearing a turquoise dress, her auburn hair like a fiery halo, walking through a field full of flowers. He wasn't sure where this image had come from unless it had been conjured up by that elusive fragrance she wore, which reminded him of summer flowers. She was there when he woke up in the mornings before he even had a chance to turn his head and look at Consuela's photograph. She was there many times during his day, hovering on the edges of his consciousness, and again at night, after his final thoughts of Consuela and in those last moments before sleep claimed him, it was that sun-filled image of Lara that he took with him into his dreams.

She was sitting at a table in the window of the crowded wine bar, her head turned so that only her profile was visible to him as he stood at the bar. It was an entrancing profile—a short straight nose, high cheekbones, long lashes and a sensual mouth above a sharp but determined jaw. That mass of hair was still drawn back from her face in the way she wore it for work and fastened at the nape of her neck with a black velvet bow. Even as he watched her Andres felt a quickening of his pulse. She was wearing her white trench coat over a black outfit—a perfect foil against her hair—and boots with slim high heels.

'Will that be all, sir?'

Andres swung back to the bar to find the barman leaning forward anxiously and his order before him on the counter. 'Oh, yes,' he said, taking out his wallet. 'Sorry.' He'd become so lost in his contemplation of Lara that momentarily he'd become oblivious of everything else around him. After paying for the drinks, he carried the two glasses of wine back to the table and set them down, telling himself as he did so to stop being so ridiculous and to get a grip on himself.

'So…' He removed his overcoat, draped it over a chair and sat down. 'How have you been getting along at the Roseberry?'

'Very well really,' Lara replied.

He laughed. 'You said that as if you were surprised, as if you hadn't been expecting to get on well.'

'Did I?' She smiled. 'I didn't mean it to sound that way. But to be honest with you, I was a bit apprehensive. I thought it would be very different from St Joseph's.'

'And is it?' he asked. 'Different from St Joseph's, I mean?'

'In some ways,' she replied slowly, 'but not in others. Let's face it, patients are patients whether they are called clients or not. They all need care and looking after, so from a nursing point of view it's not really very different.'

'In what ways do you find it different?' He lifted his glass as he spoke. 'Cheers.'

'Yes, cheers.' Lara lifted her own glass then took a sip of her wine before answering. 'Well, I suppose it's the whole private care aspect that is different, and the staffing and management is very different, of course. But I have to say you were quite right when you said the reasons for cosmetic surgery can be every bit as heart-wrenching as those for, say, a burns victim.'

'We do sometimes have some pretty frivolous and needless requests,' he said, setting his glass down and sitting back in his chair.

'How do you deal with those?' she asked curiously.

'One of the consultants will talk to the potential client at great length, and if it is felt that the client is unsuitable for surgery or if the proposed surgery is unnecessary or will not improve their confidence or quality of life in any way, they are dissuaded from pursuing their request any further.'

'I see,' Lara replied slowly.

'Tell me,' he said after a moment, 'how are the shifts working out with your home life?'

'Very well so far,' she replied. 'In fact, I think this new regime is encouraging Cassie to go out more and do more—although we have a long way to go yet. But I have to say, financially it will make a tremendous difference.' She paused. 'And we have you to thank for that.' As she spoke she threw him an almost shy glance from beneath her eyelashes.

'Not at all,' he replied. 'Don't mention it.'

'I mean it,' she said. 'We are very, very grateful to

you, and if there is ever anything we can do in return…'

He smiled and took a mouthful of his drink. As he set the glass down again an idea came unbidden into his mind. It was a crazy idea, one that really should not even be pursued, but as Lara lifted those green eyes in his direction he rapidly reached a decision. 'Actually,' he said, and she raised her eyebrows questioningly, 'maybe there is something you could do…'

'Yes?' She sounded surprised but not alarmed or unwilling so, encouraged by this, Andres took a deep breath and proceeded to explain.

'I am in something of a predicament,' he said, wondering even as he spoke whether or not this was something in which he should involve Lara who now, by his own efforts, was not only a colleague but also an employee. 'Since coming to London, friends of mine have been determined to find a partner for me.'

'Do you mean partner in the business sense or the personal sense?' A small smile played around Lara's mouth.

'Oh, the personal sense,' he replied with a sigh. 'Most definitely the personal sense.' All around them the hubbub of the wine bar carried on, and as he struggled to find the right words to explain his predicament, at the same time wishing he'd never started, Lara spoke again.

'Can I take it that you don't wish this partner to be found for you?' she asked. He stared at her and although now her expression was perfectly serious, he thought, just for a moment, that he detected a hint of mischief in her eyes.

'Yes,' he said, 'that's absolutely right. Should I ever feel the need to find a partner, I would do so on my own, but until that time I don't need anyone else to do it for me.'

'So how can I help?'

'It's a party,' he said, 'a party for Valentine's Day. And unless I can say I am taking someone with me, I know Annabel will have someone lined up for me.'

'Annabel?' asked Lara.

'Yes. Theo's wife,' he replied.

'Ah.'

'She does it all the time,' he went on miserably. 'It wasn't too bad at first but I'm really fed up with it now. I don't know where she finds some of these women—she seems to think they are my type and they most definitely are not. Anyway, it leaves me in the situation of having to let them down gently after the event. They all seem to think because we share one date we are on the way to a full-scale affair.'

'Why does she do it—Annabel?' asked Lara curiously.

'I think she feels sorry for me,' he said.

'Why should she feel sorry for you?' Lara frowned.

He was silent for a long moment during which the shrieks of laughter from a group of young women at an adjoining table jarred his nerves, unsettling him. 'My wife died five years ago,' he explained at last, 'and since then I really haven't felt the need to look for another relationship.' He paused again, aware that Lara had grown very still and was watching him carefully, as if she was oblivious to those around them. 'Annabel and some of my other friends seem to think differently,' he went on after a moment. 'They seem convinced that I can never be truly happy again until I find someone else.'

'And what do you think?' asked Lara quietly.

He shrugged. 'I know I could never find anyone to take Consuela's place,' he replied, 'so really I can't see much point in trying.' He paused, then added firmly, 'In fact, if I'm really honest, I don't want anyone to take her place.'

'And where do I come into all this?' she asked leaning back slightly in her chair.

Andres took a deep breath. 'I was wondering,' he said, 'if you would consider accompanying me to this Valentine dinner party—no strings attached, of course.'

'Of course,' said Lara. She spoke seriously, but for the fraction of a second Andres once again had the feeling that she might be mocking him—ever so gently, but mocking nevertheless. He found himself wishing he'd never started this particular conversation.

'Yes, all right,' she said suddenly.

'Ycs…?' He stared at her, not convinced that she was actually agreeing to anything.

'Yes, I'll come with you.'

'You'll…?' He stared at her, unable to believe what she had said. When she smiled and nodded, it was his turn to lean back in his chair. 'Thank you, Lara,' he said, and he knew there was a note of relief in his voice and that she must have heard it. 'That's great and it's really very good of you.'

'Not at all.' She gave a little laugh. 'It's the least I can do. Like I say, it'll be a way I can show my gratitude for the job.'

He could hardly believe it. He'd asked her on the spur of the moment, not thinking she'd agree, especially under the circumstances which were a bit bizarre to say the least. Yet here she was, not only apparently understanding his reasons for asking her but also agreeing to his request. And suddenly he found himself actually looking forward to the evening, which until that moment he had been dreading. He was looking forward to telling Annabel that he would be bringing someone with him, he was looking forward to seeing Theo's face when he realised that his partner for the evening was Lara, someone whom Theo himself had described as a stunner. But more than any of those reasons, he found that he was looking forward to actually taking Lara there and having her at his side.

'Tell me about your wife,' said Lara suddenly, breaking into his thoughts.

He was surprised, shocked even. No one, but no one ever mentioned Consuela these days. In fact, he couldn't remember the last time he had spoken about her. 'What do you want to know?' he asked warily.

'What was her name?' Lara leaned forward slightly and he caught the summer meadow scent. 'And how did you meet?'

He hesitated, took another mouthful of wine, then said, 'Her name was Consuela.'

'What a lovely name.' Lara nodded, encouraging him to continue.

'We more or less grew up together in our home town of Cordoba—our families were friends. We trained at medical school together after I'd finished my education in this country. Everyone expected us to marry.'

'And you didn't disappoint them?'

'No.' A far-away look came into his eyes as momentarily, in his thoughts, he returned to the country of his birth. 'We were married by the bishop in the cathedral in Cordoba. Afterwards we lived in Buenos Aires, where we both had jobs in the city's main hospital.'

'Did you have any children?' Lara asked gently.

'No.' He shook his head. 'We both wanted children but it never happened—we were on the verge of seeking reasons for this when…when Consuela fell sick.'

'What was it?' asked Lara.

Again he was surprised by her bluntness—no one had ever questioned him about his wife in this way. Usually when they heard she was dead they simply mumbled that they were sorry and never returned to the subject again. 'Leukaemia,' he said. 'She had the best available treatment—I even took her to Scandinavia to a clinic that was pioneering a new treatment, but it was no good…' He felt his throat tighten as those terrible, dark days came back in sudden, gut-wrenching detail. 'She died at the family home in Cordoba.'

'Is she buried there?' asked Lara.

He threw her a sharp glance, once more startled by her question, but all he saw in her face was compassion, not curiosity. He swallowed. 'Yes,' he said at last. 'We held the funeral at the cathedral…'

'Where you were married.'

'Yes,' he confirmed, 'where we were married.' He swallowed, trying to control his emotions, then after a moment he was able to continue. 'All I could see that day was a sea of white lilies…then…Consuela was laid to rest in the family plot in Cordoba.'

'Tell me what she was like,' Lara went on. 'What did she look like?'

Andres drew in his breath sharply, not sure he was able to continue with this particular turn the conversation had taken.

'Was she dark and Spanish-looking—like you?' Lara went on relentlessly.

'Yes,' he said, 'yes, she was. She was tall and very

slim with long black hair and very dark eyes.' He paused, considering, as memories flooded his mind. 'She had the most incredible laugh—infectious, you know what I mean? But she could also be fiery—she was hot-blooded and very passionate about issues that concerned her. She loved animals,' he went on, warming to the theme now. 'Her family kept horses just as mine did and we would ride out together across the pampas…' He paused again, remembering. 'She also liked to dance,' he went on after a moment. 'She loved the tango which, of course, is our national dance, and the salsa.'

'She sounds a lovely lady,' said Lara.

'Yes,' he said, 'she was…' He trailed off, finding it impossible to continue any further.

'So these friends of yours—did they know Consuela?' Lara sounded curious now.

'Well,' he considered, 'Theo and Annabel had met her certainly, but they didn't know her very well. I met Theo at school and later we were at Oxford together. They came to our wedding…'

'So they must surely know that these women they try to pair you up with are nothing like Consuela and consequently not your type?'

'You'd think so, wouldn't you?' He pulled a face. 'But nothing seems to deter them, especially Annabel. Still, maybe this time if you come with me it will be different. At least it will prove to them that I am perfectly capable of finding my own partner and don't need any help from them.' He paused as a thought suddenly struck him. 'I hope I won't be intruding on anyone?'

Lara frowned. 'What do you mean?'

'Well, there isn't some irate boyfriend of yours who will get the wrong end of the stick?'

'Oh, no,' she said quickly, 'there's no one like that in my life at the moment.'

He was aware of a surge of something at her words—whether relief or pleasure, he wasn't sure. 'I can hardly believe that,' he said. 'I felt sure there would be someone.'

'There was,' she admitted slowly, staring down into her glass.

'What happened?' he said gently.

'It ended.' She shrugged. 'These things happen.'

'I'm sorry,' he said, noting a little flash of pain in her eyes.

'I guess he simply couldn't cope with my domestic arrangements,' she said. 'Let's face it, it isn't every man who could accept an invalid sister and three young children, is it?'

'No,' Andres agreed. 'I guess that would put intolerable strain on any relationship, especially if you weren't heavily committed in the first place.' He hoped he sounded sympathetic but privately he thought it must have been a pretty shallow sort of man who had been unable to cope with a few of life's problems. 'Who was he?' he asked after a moment, wondering if it might be someone from St Joseph's.

'A doctor,' she replied. 'He was Swedish; his name was Sven. I thought I was in love with him at the time. Now I doubt it was love.'

'Does he work at St Joseph's?' he asked.

'No.' Lara shook her head and again he saw that little flash of pain and knew she had been hurt. 'He's gone back to Sweden.'

'I see.' He paused. 'Can I get you another drink?' he asked.

She shook her head. 'No, thank you,' she said. 'I really should be getting home.'

'In that case…' He stood up. 'I'll walk you back to your car.'

As they returned to the car park of the Roseberry and he saw Lara into her car and watched her drive away, Andres was aware of a lifting of his spirits. When he tried to analyse the reason he came to the conclusion that it was as if by merely talking about Consuela to someone who hadn't actually known her, a corner of that curtain of darkness that had fallen over him on the day she had died and had remained there ever since had lifted, ever so slightly, and had allowed in the light.

## CHAPTER SEVEN

'BUT what in the world am I going to wear?' It was the following day and Lara had just told Cassie about the Valentine's Day party. Cassie predictably showed great interest.

'I told you, didn't I?' she said, clasping her hands together. 'I knew he was interested in you.'

'Don't get too excited,' Lara replied dryly. 'It isn't quite what you think.'

'Oh?' Cassie frowned. 'What do you mean?'

'He's only asked me to keep his friends from dragging along some other woman for him.'

'But would they do that?' Cassie seemed bemused at the idea.

'Apparently it appears they've done it before.' Lara chuckled. 'On several occasions. And as far as Andres is concerned, these women simply aren't his type.'

'Which suggests that he considers that you are,' Cassie mused slowly.

'Not necessarily,' Lara replied lightly, although her heart missed a beat at such a possibility. 'It merely means that this way he can take someone he already knows...'

'What sort of party is it?' asked Cassie.

'Do you know? I'm not really sure.' Lara shook her head. 'I was so amazed when he asked me that I forgot to ask.'

'I think you need to find out.'

'To be honest, it won't make a lot of difference.'

Lara sighed. 'It'll have to be something I've already got. I can't afford anything new and that's that.'

'I have that little black dress I bought for that last work do of Dave's and never wore because we didn't go...' Cassie trailed off.

'I couldn't wear that,' Lara protested quickly, remembering that Cassie hadn't gone because of her accident.

'I don't see why not.' Cassie sniffed. 'It cost me an arm and a leg at the time and it's been sitting there in the wardrobe ever since, and I'm not likely to wear it in the foreseeable future.'

'You never know,' Lara replied stoutly, but Cassie cut her short.

'Come on, Lara, be realistic. When am I likely to go anywhere to wear anything like that again? The dress hasn't dated, it's a classic design, and you and I are more or less the same size. Check up and make sure it's appropriate...'

'I'm sure it would be,' Lara murmured.

'You never know—it could be a fancy-dress party or something, being Valentine's Day. But if it isn't, I would be only too happy for you to wear it.'

'Thanks, Cass.' Lara gave her sister a quick hug. 'That's really kind of you.'

'Not at all,' said Cassie, 'it'll be nice to do something for you for a change.' She paused. 'What I don't understand is why should Andres's friends feel the need to keep trying to find a partner for him?'

'They feel sorry for him apparently.'

'Why?' Cassie frowned.

'Remember I told you his wife died?' said Lara. 'Well, it appears his friends seem to think he should have got over her death by now and should be moving on—they think that by finding the right partner for him they would be helping him to do that.'

'And has he got over her death yet?'

Lara shrugged. 'I don't think so. I guess I don't know him well enough to say for sure, but by talking to him I got the impression her death is still pretty raw for him.'

'How long is it since she died?'

'Five years, but they grew up together, were childhood sweethearts, in fact, so she had always been an important part of his life. I rather got the impression that he hasn't been able to talk about her since her death.'

'You mean because he finds it too painful or because people avoid the issue?' Cassie's frown deepened.

'A bit of both really, I think,' Lara replied. 'I don't think he wants anyone else in his life. If someone has been such an important part of your life as his wife was, I guess you can't just blot them out.'

'I know,' said Cassie quietly. 'I'm finding that.'

'Oh, Cass, I'm sorry.' Lara stared at her sister and saw her face crumple around the edges of her scars. 'You mean Dave?'

Cassie nodded. 'Most of the time I'm still so angry with him that I don't want to talk about him, but at other times memories creep back in—happy memories, good times we had with the children, that sort of thing—and, well, it's very hard.'

'I'm sure it is,' Lara replied gently. She hesitated. 'Has Callum said any more about him being at the school?' she asked after a moment.

Cassie shook her head. 'No,' she said slowly, 'although I did think I saw him myself a couple of days ago. It was only a back view and I couldn't be sure...'

'Do you think he wants to make contact?' asked Lara.

'I don't know.' Cassie shook her head and Lara saw a single tear run down the side of her face. 'I'm sure he must be missing the children—he thought the world of them, you know.'

'Yes, I know he did,' Lara agreed.

'Anyway.' Cassie stood up briskly. 'That's another story. We were talking about you and this wonderful new man that's come into your life.'

'Cassie, it's hardly that,' Lara protested. 'I'm simply doing him a favour, that's all—a favour in return for him getting me the job at the Roseberry.'

'Yes, all right,' said Cassie, moving to the door. 'We'll see.'

'Annabel? It's Andres.'

'Andres! How are you? Theo and I were only talking about you last night, darling.'

'Nice things, I hope?'

'But of course—always nice things about you.'

'That's comforting. Annabel, about this party of yours for Valentine's Day…'

'Yes? Oh, darling, don't say you aren't coming.'

'No, on the contrary.'

'Thank heavens for that. Why, I was only saying to Theo that we don't see nearly enough of you. Now, listen, for this party—'

'Actually, Annabel,' he interrupted before she could go any further, 'I phoned to make a request about the party.'

'Oh?'

'Yes, not to say that I wasn't able to come but rather to ask you if I could bring someone with me.' In the silence that followed his request Andres could picture Annabel's face perfectly, her expression a mixture of amazement and possibly irritation at having to rearrange her seating plan and maybe even the guest list itself.

'But of course, darling,' she said at last, as her years of training at being the perfect hostess came rapidly to the fore. 'We will be absolutely delighted. But tell me, who is she? Is she anyone we know? I must say, you've kept very quiet about this.'

'Her name is Lara.'

'What a lovely name,' Annabel replied. 'Shades of *Doctor Zhivago* and all that.'

'Yes, quite,' he agreed, 'but I don't think you would know her, although Theo has met her.'

'Really! He never said. I can see I will have to have words with that husband of mine. What is Lara's surname?'

'Gregory,' Andres replied, wondering as he said it if he was doing the right thing in catapulting Lara into something she might not enjoy.

'Gregory?' mused Annabel. 'Any relation to Sir Michael Gregory?'

'I have no idea,' Andres replied, 'but it's all right for me to bring her to the party?'

'Of course, it is,' Annabel replied. 'We shall be enchanted to meet her.'

'That's great. Oh, Annabel, just one other thing. Exactly what sort of party is it—dress and all that?'

'Oh, black tie, darling. Sorry, didn't Theo say? Drinks first at seven, here in Chelsea, followed by dinner at eight, then on to a club.'

'That's great, Annabel—just as long as I know.'

* * *

Lara wasn't sure how she felt about going to the party with Andres. She had been only too pleased to be able to do something in return to thank him for the trouble he'd gone to on her behalf over the job at the Roseberry, and while there was a part of her that tingled with excitement whenever she thought about the event there was another part—possibly the greater—that was filled with apprehension whenever it came into her mind.

She knew none of these friends of his other than Theo McFarlane, whom she'd met only briefly, but no doubt they would all be wealthy and from the upper strata of society. Not that that in itself bothered Lara. She had always felt she could hold her head high in any circle. And now that Cassie, bless her, had solved the problem over what she should wear, another anxiety had been removed—always supposing, of course, it was the type of party where a little black dress would be appropriate. So what was it that was bothering her? What was it that caused her heart to lurch almost in fear whenever she thought about it? She wasn't really sure. She only knew it was the same mixture of emotions she felt whenever she knew she was about to see Andres, whether at the Roseberry or at St Joseph's.

She had no chance for a private word with him as to the exact nature of the party until one morning at St Joseph's at the end of a busy theatre list during which four patients had undergone skin grafts following accidents in which they had received severe burns. Still clad in his theatre greens and white boots and with the red cap on his head, he was standing at the nurses' station, discussing post-operative care with Tom Martin and Sue Jackman. Lara, watching from the ward where she had just finished carrying out half-hourly observations on those patients who'd undergone surgery that morning, picked her moment carefully, moving forward as Sue went back into her office and Tom walked off down the corridor.

'Andres,' she said softly, 'may I have a word?'

He was studying a report but he looked round quickly as she approached. 'Of course,' he said. Did his expression soften when he saw her or did she imagine it?

'I've been wondering,' she said in the same quiet tone, ensuring that only he would hear her, 'about the party...'

'Yes?' There was amusement in his eyes now. 'Don't tell me, you've decided you don't want to come after all. Well, I can't say I blame you...'

'Oh, no,' she said quickly, 'it's nothing like that—really.'

'Really?' The dark eyebrows rose in surprise. 'Like I say, I wouldn't blame you.'

'No,' she said, 'I'm still coming—that is, if you want me to—but I was wondering what sort of party it is.'

'I understand there will be drinks first—cocktails,' he said, 'then dinner, then there's talk of going on to a club.'

'Oh, that's all right,' she said in relief as she thought of the little black dress hanging in Cassie's wardrobe, knowing it would be entirely suitable for what he was describing.

'I've checked the rotas at the Roseberry,' he said, 'and I see that you are on duty that afternoon. You won't have time to go home to change so maybe you would like to come to my house to get ready?'

'Oh.' She stared at him. 'Thank you,' she added weakly, not knowing quite what else to say.

'Afterwards, I will arrange for a car to take you home,' he said. 'Is that all right?'

'Oh, yes, of course.' For some reason her heart was thumping even more than it usually did when she encountered him. She only hoped he couldn't hear it. She didn't know why she should react in this way because the one thing she really had to remember was that she mustn't allow her head to be turned by all this talk of dinners and clubs. This was purely an arrangement between the two of them, nothing more, nothing less, an arrangement to put paid to the matchmaking tendencies of Andres's over-enthusiastic friends.

'I have to go now.' He glanced at the clock over the nurses' station. 'I have a clinic to take in Harley Street this afternoon.' His voice softened slightly. 'I'll see you soon, Lara.'

'Yes,' she replied breathlessly, 'see you soon.' She watched him walk away, feeling so overwhelmed she thought shc might bc about to burst.

'Lara!' She jumped guiltily and turned to find Sue in the doorway of her office. 'Would you come in here for a moment, please?'

This was it, she thought miserably as she followed Sue into the room and waited while the sister firmly closed the door.

'It's come to my notice,' said Sue, sitting down behind her desk and coming straight to the point, 'that you have taken on another job. Is that correct?'

'Yes, it is.' Lara straightened her shoulders and looked Sue squarely in the eye.

'May I ask why?' she asked coolly.

'Because I need the money.'

'You know how I feel about moonlighting,' Sue went on.

'It's hardly that,' Lara interrupted her. 'I'm only part time here, a situation that was forced on me by my home circumstances. I now find myself in a position of needing more hours, and if you remember rightly, I approached you first to see if more hours were available on this unit. You told me there weren't—'

'I also told you that there would eventually be another post coming up—that staff are coming and going all the time.'

'I wasn't financially in a position to wait,' Lara protested. 'So when I was offered another job, a job which, I may add, fitted in perfectly and in no way threatened my hours here—'

'You grabbed it.'

'Well, I wouldn't exactly put it like that,' Lara retorted, 'but when Andr—Mr Ricardo,' she corrected herself quickly, but not before she'd seen the expression that flitted across the other woman's face, 'suggested I attend an interview at the Roseberry clinic, I agreed.'

'How did he know you were looking for another job?' demanded Sue.

'He happened to overhear the conversation you and I had when I asked you for more hours and you told me there were none.'

'So it was nothing to do with you offering him lifts in your car—or anything else for that matter?'

Lara stared at her. 'No, of course not!' she said, feeling the colour rush to her face. 'What do you take me for?'

Sue shrugged. 'In my experience, Lara, men are men and they can rarely resist anything that is on offer.'

'I can assure you there was nothing on offer,' said Lara hotly.

'Maybe not, but by the same token where men are concerned there is no such thing as a free lunch. If he's done you a favour, he'll expect one back.'

'I'm more than capable of taking care of myself,' retorted Lara.

'So what was all that about just now?' Sue's eyes had narrowed suspiciously, and in spite of her anger Lara was reminded what Katie had told her about the sister fancying the new consultant locum.

'What was all what about?' she demanded.

'You and Mr Ricardo with your heads together, whispering in a corner.'

'We were not whispering,' she retorted angrily.

'So what were you doing?'

'We...we were discussing a patient.' It was a white lie and she knew it, but in view of what had just been said, Lara couldn't bring herself to tell Sue what she and Andres had really been discussing.

'Well, I hope it was one of our patients here at St Joseph's,' Sue said acidly, 'and not one of the patients at the Roseberry Clinic. I can't pretend I'm happy about this arrangement,' she went on in the same acerbic tones, 'but I don't suppose there's a lot I can do about it.'

Moments later, still smarting from Sue's words, Lara found herself back on the ward. Katie had just received a delivery of dressings and other goods from hospital stores and was in the process of carrying them from the nurses' station to the ward's small storeroom. She looked up as Lara approached. 'What's up?' she said, catching sight of her friend's expression and pausing in her work, her arms full of packages.

'I've just had an ear-bashing from our Reverend Sister,' Lara replied, pulling a face and resorting to the nickname that had been given to Sue on more than one occasion.

'Oh?' Katie raised her eyebrows. 'What about?'

'My moonlighting, as she puts it,' Lara replied through gritted teeth.

'Your moonlighting?' Katie stared at her, then as it dawned on her what Lara meant, she gave a chuckle. 'Oh,' she said, 'I see. Well, you can rest assured it will have less to do with what you are actually doing than where it is and who made it possible.'

'Yes.' Lara drew in her breath sharply. 'I guess you're right.'

'I told you she fancied him, didn't I?' said Katie with a little hint of triumph in her tone.

'Yes, you did,' Lara agreed, picking up a stack of packets of gauze squares and carrying them into the storeroom. 'She won't get anywhere with him, though.'

'I certainly wouldn't think she was his type,' said Katie, following her into the room. 'Not in a million years.'

'I didn't actually mean that.' Lara turned from the shelf.

'What did you mean?' Katie frowned.

'I don't think he's over the death of his wife yet, and because of that he isn't interested in starting a relationship with anyone.'

Katie stared at her. 'How in the world have you reached that conclusion?' she asked in amazement.

'Oh, nothing really,' Lara mumbled, suddenly aware that she might have divulged too much, even to Katie who was her closest friend at St Joseph's. She had already made up her mind to say nothing of her Valentine's Day arrangement with their locum consultant.

'No, go on.' Katie obviously had other ideas and pushed the door to behind them so there would be no danger of them being overheard. 'How do you know all that? Did he tell you himself?'

Lara took a deep breath, knowing that she was cornered. 'Yes, he did,' she admitted at last.

'When did all this happen?' Katie was agog now. 'Surely not over the operating table at the Roseberry?'

'Not exactly, no…' Lara hesitated, uncertain just how much to divulge.

'Where, then?' Katie could be tenacious at the best of times, and Lara knew there was no chance she was going to give up over this.

'We went for a drink after work.'

'Aha! Now we're getting somewhere.'

'It was only a drink,' Lara protested.

'And yet he got round to telling you that he hadn't yet got over the death of his wife sufficiently to be in another relationship?' Katie sounded incredulous now, and Lara knew she would have a battle on her hands to convince her otherwise.

'It wasn't like that…' she began hesitantly.

'Come on, tell me, what was it like?' Katie raised her eyebrows.

'I'm not sure I want to talk about it.'

'Not even to me?' Katie sounded hurt. 'I thought I was your friend.'

'Oh, you are, of course you are,' sighed Lara. 'But if I tell you, I want you to promise you won't go reading more into it than there is.'

'You tell me and I'll be the judge of that.' Katie grinned.

Lara took a deep breath then went on to explain to Katie all about the party, where it was and why Andres wanted her to go with him. 'He simply doesn't want another relationship,' she ended up.

'Told you that as well, did he?' asked Katie, with more than a trace of scepticism in her voice.

'Not in so many words, no, but it's the impression I gained from hearing him talk.'

'OK, right, so he's taking you to this party to keep these friends quiet and that's the only reason?'

'Well, yes…'

'And you're happy with that?' Katie's voice softened slightly and in the background on the ward Lara was vaguely aware of some sort of commotion.

'Yes,' she declared passionately. 'I felt it was the least I could do after him getting me the job at the Roseberry. Surely there's nothing wrong with that? Honestly, Katie, you're beginning to sound like Cassie.'

'You mean she thinks there must be more to it as well?'

'Oh, I don't know!' Lara turned away in growing exasperation, wishing she'd never attempted to explain anything to Katie.

'So where is it—this party?' Katie obviously hadn't finished.

'Somewhere in Chelsea, I think.' Lara kept her tone deliberately vague.

'And what is it exactly?'

'What do you mean, what is it?' she hedged. 'It's just a party.'

'Drinks? Buffet? Bring a bottle?'

'Dinner party, actually.'

'My, my, dinner party in Chelsea.' Katie's eyes widened. 'That's a bit of a far cry from our usual spag bol and a bottle, isn't it?'

Lara remained silent and Katie lowered her head in order to be able to look into her face. 'And when did you say it is?'

'I didn't say…but it's the fourteenth.'

'Of *this* month?'

'Yes.'

'Oh, boy! And you're trying to pretend there's nothing in it? St Valentine's Day? Pull the other one, Lara. He's got a thing about you, you mark my words. He may have implied he doesn't want another relationship yet but—' Katie broke off as the storeroom door was suddenly flung open.

'What in the world is going on in here?' Sue stood in the open doorway, glaring at Katie and Lara. 'I've been calling the pair of you.'

'Sorry, Sue,' said Katie sweetly. 'We've been putting the stores away, haven't we, Lara?'

'Hmm, gossiping more likely,' said Sue with a sniff. 'Well, for your information, we have an emergency just come up from A and E, and I need you both on the ward.'

'Right,' said Katie calmly, 'we're coming.'

They followed the sister back onto the ward where they found the emergency patient was being transferred from the porter's trolley to a bed in a single side bay.

'This is Mary Taylor,' said Sue, taking up the notes of the patient and reading out the history. 'She received twenty per cent burns in a kitchen fire at her home this morning. She has been stabilised in A and E and is receiving intravenous fluids and analgesics to help control her pain. She has superficial burns on her arms, partial-thickness burns on her face and hands and several patches of full-thickness burns also on her face and hands. Mr Ricardo fortunately hasn't left the hospital yet so he said he will come and see her before he goes.'

The following half-hour was spent making Mary Taylor as comfortable as possible. Understandably she had become distraught by her condition and consequently had been given sedatives in A and E, from which she was still extremely drowsy. By the time Lara had inserted a catheter Andres had arrived on the ward. Quietly he approached the patient's bedside and gently touched a part of her arm that hadn't been injured.

'Hello, Mary,' he said softly. It was unlikely that she heard him, though if she did she would probably be unable to concentrate or understand what he said, but in spite of that Andres continued talking in the same gentle tone. 'I don't want to disturb you too much but I'm going to take a look at your burns.'

Mary opened her eyes and moaned softly.

Gently, carefully, with Lara's assistance Andres examined the raw, inflamed patches on the woman's face, arms and hands. 'I think,' he said, still addressing his comments to the patient, 'that in time I will be able to make you as good as new, but for now I just want you to rest and not to worry about a thing.' Straightening up, he turned to Lara and indicated for her to replace the light gauze dressings on Mary's wounds. At that moment a man appeared at the entrance to the bay accompanied by Jill Bryan, one of the unit's health support workers.

'This is Mr Taylor,' Jill explained, looking from Lara and Katie to Andres Ricardo then back to Lara again. 'Mrs Taylor's husband.'

'Mary…' The man would have rushed forward and possibly embraced his wife, oblivious to her injuries, but Andres restrained him with a firm hand on his arm.

'Careful,' he said. 'She has serious burns.'

'Oh, Mary.' The man stared helplessly down at his wife who, apart from a slight flicker of her eyelashes, hardly seemed aware of his presence. 'How in the world did this happen?' Looking up at the staff who were present in the bay, he appealed to them. 'Do any of you know what happened?'

'Only that there was a fire in the kitchen of your home,' Sue replied, 'and that your wife sustained serious burns to her hands, face and arms. I'm sure you will be able to receive a fuller report from the fire officers who attended the incident.'

'So what happens now?' the man appealed helplessly.

'Well, your wife will remain on the unit for some time until some of her burns have healed—the rest will require some skin grafting.'

'Skin grafts!' The man looked shocked.

'Yes.' Sue turned to Andres. 'This is Mr Ricardo, our consultant surgeon. He will be carrying out any skin grafts that your wife may require.'

Mr Taylor turned to Andres. 'When will you be doing all this?' he asked in bewilderment.

'Not immediately,' Andres replied. 'We need to give your wife a little time to recover, but when I feel the time is right I will commence with some grafting.'

'But what happens with this grafting?' Mr Taylor still looked confused. 'Where do you get the skin from? Does it come from someone else—like a transplant?'

'No.' Andres shook his head. 'We take some healthy skin from another site on your wife's body—there is much less possibility of rejection that way—possibly from her inner thigh. If that is not possible, maybe from inside her upper arm.'

'And what if you don't do that?'

'There will be extensive scarring,' Andres replied quietly.

'Oh, God.' The man sank down onto a chair and held his head in his hands. 'I can't take all this in.'

Lara stepped forward and touched his shoulder lightly. 'Is there someone we could call for you?' she said gently. 'A relative or perhaps a friend who could be with you at this time?'

Mr Taylor looked up and through the mists of his confusion there appeared a slight glimmer, as he understood what Lara was saying. 'My daughter,' he said at last. 'She should know about this.'

'Does she live close by?' asked Lara.

'Yes. Well, about half an hour away by car.'

'In that case, I suggest you phone her, or if you like we could phone her. I'm sure she would want to be here with her mother.'

'Yes, all right.' The man stood up, 'I'll phone her,' he muttered.

'Come into my office,' said Sue. 'You can phone from there.'

Together Sue and Mr Taylor left the bay for Sue's office, leaving Lara, Katie and Andres at Mary's bedside.

'I have to go,' said Andres after a moment. 'That is, if you don't need me here any longer.'

'No, I don't think so.' It was Katie who answered, a suddenly very alert Katie who seemed to be watching for any interaction between Lara and Andres.

'I need to get back to London,' he went on, apparently mercifully oblivious to Katie's heightened interest. 'I have a clinic this afternoon.' He paused and his gaze met Lara's. 'I'll see you in a couple of days' time, Lara.'

'Yes.' She swallowed. A couple of days' time was the next time she had a shift at the Roseberry. It was also the fourteenth of February—the date of the dinner party and St Valentine's Day. 'Yes, of course.'

He'd barely left the bay when Katie gave a snort of laughter. 'You're trying to tell me there's nothing in it?' She chortled. 'That him taking you to this party is purely and simply to shut his friends up?'

'Yes,' Lara began indignantly, but Katie cut her short.

'Rubbish,' she said. 'Pull the other one. Honestly, Lara, do you think I was born yesterday?'

'I don't know what you mean,' said Lara almost primly, but deep down her heart was doing incredible gymnastics at the look that had been in Andres's eyes when he'd looked at her.

'Yes, you do,' said Katie. 'And if you don't, you should have been standing where I was. Honestly, Lara, the way he looked at you…'

'Don't be silly,' Lara protested. 'I told you this party is an arrangement, nothing more than that.'

'Huh,' said Katie. 'Believe that and you'll believe anything. I'd love to be a fly on the wall or failing that…' she chuckled '…I'd dearly love to be around when our Reverend Sister finds out about it.'

'Don't.' Lara shuddered. 'I'm hoping she never will.'

'I shouldn't count on it,' Katie replied, 'I have a strong feeling that pretty soon everyone will know about you and Andres Ricardo, and that includes Sue Jackman.'

## CHAPTER EIGHT

IT HAD been a busy shift at the Roseberry, with a full operating list and post-operative care, but in spite of that Lara had found it difficult to concentrate with the prospect of that evening's dinner party crowding her mind at every opportunity. At last, however, the shift was over and Andres met her in Reception, where he had arranged for a cab to pick them up and take them to his home.

Her heart was thumping with excitement as she sat beside him in the back of the cab, and as they drew out into the London traffic she had to remind herself more than once that this was purely an arrangement and she would do well to put any of the notions that either Cassie or Katie might have had firmly out of her mind. The traffic was heavy and it took almost half an hour to reach Andres's home in Knightsbridge, but at last the cab entered the secluded square and drew to a halt before a tall, imposing building of red brick. Andres helped her from the cab, paid the driver then picked up her bag, while Lara carried the plastic cover that contained her dress and followed him up the short flight of steps to the front door.

In the large hallway, with its black and white tiled floor, she waited while Andres de-activated the alarm system.

'Perhaps you'd like to come up to a room where you can change?' he said.

She followed him up a wide staircase with black and

gilt wrought-iron banisters to a gallery overlooking the stairs and the hall below. Above them two crystal chandeliers glittered as brightly as polished diamonds, while beneath them their feet sank into the soft pile of a carpet of Chinese design.

Andres had been mostly silent on the drive from the Roseberry and Lara had found herself wondering more than once if he was regretting arranging the rather odd circumstances for this evening. She had begun to wonder about it herself, for while she had accepted his reasons for asking her at the time, she had since found herself wondering what would happen afterwards. Even if his friends did accept the fact that he had someone in his life again, they would surely realise the truth when she was no longer in evidence. Or maybe his sole purpose was simply to let these friends know that he was perfectly capable of arranging his own affairs in the future.

The room he showed her into was beautifully furnished in rich dark wood, its décor in shades of cream and lemon in perfect contrast, and with its own *en suite* bathroom. It overlooked a walled garden at the rear of the house.

'This is lovely,' she said, gazing out of the window.

'I'll leave you to get ready,' he said. 'If there is anything else you need, I'll be downstairs.'

After he had gone she unpacked the few items she'd brought with her—toiletries and make-up, her evening shoes and bag and the aquamarine pashmina her father had given her for her birthday a couple of years previously and which she knew suited her colouring but which she'd had little occasion to wear. She took a leisurely, scented bath and washed her hair, then while it was drying she applied her make-up—a little more than she usually wore—accentuating her eyes with misty grey and her lashes with mascara, highlighting her cheekbones with soft blusher and her lips with matching colour. With silk underwear and sheer stockings, she was at last ready to step into the black dress, drawing it up over her body and onto her shoulders, the sensuous folds of the material caressing her skin.

Her hair she left loose, allowing it to dry into its natural fiery mass of curls and tendrils. Her only jewellery was a drop diamanté pendant on a gold chain, matching earrings and a slim gold bracelet, which she slipped onto her wrist before spraying herself with the light floral perfume she always wore. As she carried out these tasks she found herself wondering about Consuela and whether she had stood in this very room, getting ready to go out with her husband. Her death had been tragic at such a young age and ever since Andres had told her about his wife, Lara had often thought about the beautiful Argentinean woman he had loved and lost.

With her own fair complexion, green eyes and auburn curls, Lara knew she was the very opposite in appearance to Consuela and she could well imagine the comment and speculation this would cause among his friends. As she gazed at her reflection in a full-length mirror she knew not only the apprehension she'd felt about that evening since the moment Andres had asked her but a moment of pure panic.

What if they didn't like her—thought her wholly unsuitable for Andres both in her appearance and her background? But if they did—did it matter? Did any of it matter? This whole thing was merely a charade, a pretence that she was required to keep up simply for that one evening. Surely she could manage that? Her reflection stared solemnly back at her. Of course she could—it was the least she could do for Andres, whose actions had all but resolved her financial predicament. Straightening her shoulders, she took a deep breath and, fastening a smile on her face, left the room and slowly descended the staircase.

Andres was standing below in the hallway, and for a brief moment before he knew she was there she was able to observe him. She had always thought he cut an imposing figure, whether at work in his white coat or theatre greens or outdoors in the long overcoat and black fedora in which he had first attracted her attention. But now, at the sight of him in evening dress, he looked so arrestingly handsome that her breath caught in her throat. Something must have told him she was there for at that moment he looked up, and as their eyes met briefly she paused, one hand on the banisters. His gaze travelled over her, taking in every detail, from Cassie's little black dress to the wild cloud of her hair, the pashmina she carried over her arm and her high-heeled evening shoes with their jewelled straps. If Lara had had doubts about her appearance, they were dispelled in that instant for the look in Andres's eyes was one of pure admiration, further borne out by his words. 'You look lovely, Lara,' he said simply.

She joined him in the hallway and he led the way into a room which, with its antique furniture and comfortable sofas, was clearly the drawing room. On a low coffee-table in front of the elegant fireplace stood a silver tray with two glasses and an ice bucket containing a bottle of champagne.

'I thought,' he said, 'a drink before we go might help to set the tone for the evening. What do you think?'

'A lovely idea,' murmured Lara, who with every

passing moment was becoming more and more convinced that she had stepped into another world—from the elegant town house in the quiet, tree-lined square in Knightsbridge, with its antiques and treasures, to drinking the most expensive champagne before embarking on an evening out, all of which could not be further removed from her own life in the tiny terraced house in Byfield.

'This…this is a beautiful house,' she said, as she watched him pour the champagne.

'It is,' he agreed. 'It's been in my mother's family for a very long time.'

'Does she come here very often?' she asked as she took the flute he passed to her.

'Not these days.' He shook his head. 'She suffers from rheumatoid arthritis and much prefers the climate of Argentina to that of London. And since my father died she is not so keen on travel as she used to be.' He lifted his glass. 'To an enjoyable evening,' he said.

'Yes,' she agreed, raising her own glass, 'an enjoyable evening.'

They both took sips then Andres said, 'I hope you'll enjoy it, Lara—that it won't be too boring for you, not knowing anyone.'

'I know you,' she said.

He stared at her. 'Yes,' he said at last, 'of course you do. And, Lara?' He paused, his gaze searching.

'Yes?'

'I would like us to appear as an item tonight, a couple, not merely that you are my date for the evening.' He paused again. 'Will that be a problem?'

She swallowed her champagne, which she had held in her mouth, hardly daring to even breathe let alone swallow while she'd waited to see what he was going to say. 'Of course not,' she said at last, her eyes watering as the bubbles fizzed in her nose.

'Good.' He replied, almost briskly, she thought, as if he was discussing the finer details of a business agreement instead of an evening out—which, when she really thought about it, was exactly what it was. She might have been happier to think of it as her doing a favour for him as a friend but, in fact, it really was a transaction in repayment for him securing the post for her at the Roseberry. The thought depressed her slightly and she took another sip of champagne before perching uneasily on the edge of the sofa and setting her glass down on the coffee-table.

They talked of other things—Callum's football team and the fact that Cassie had taken the children to visit her and Lara's parents that day.

'Where do they live?' asked Andres, and Lara decided that he really wanted to know and wasn't merely being polite.

'In a little village on the South Coast,' she replied. 'My father worked in a boatyard up until his retirement about five years ago. He and my mother live in a small cottage now, but Dad still has a boat and enjoys fishing and pottering about.'

'It sounds idyllic.' Andres smiled then lifted his head as the doorbell rang. 'That will be our cab. Are you ready?'

'Yes, of course.' She set her glass down, stood up and with her pulse suddenly racing followed him out of the room.

The cab took them to Chelsea and drew up in front of yet another elegant town house, this time the one belonging to Theo and Annabel. As Lara stepped from the taxi and Andres took her arm, she glanced up and in the first-floor windows of the house saw yet more lighted crystal chandeliers. Moments later a uniformed doorman was ushering them into the house and up a wide, sweeping staircase to the first-floor reception rooms where Theo and Annabel were waiting to receive them, Theo handsome in evening dress and his wife a tall, willowy blonde in a sea-green dress that shimmered as she moved.

'Hello, Andres, old man.' Theo gripped Andres's hand in a hearty handshake then turned to Lara. 'Lara,' he said. 'Lovely to see you, and welcome to our home.' Turning to his wife, he said, 'This is my wife, Annabel, whom I don't believe you've met. Annabel, darling, this is Lara Gregory.'

'Lara, at last,' murmured Annabel. 'I seem to have been the only one who hasn't met you.' Briefly she touched Lara's hand then turning to Andres, kissed him on the cheek, 'Dark horse,' she murmured, and led them through to meet other guests who were already assembled in the gracious reception rooms of her home.

At first Lara was bewildered by the names and struggled to remember who was who, but gradually she relaxed, helped no doubt by the champagne she'd had before leaving Andres's home, the cocktails that were being served at the McFarlanes' and the fact that as they moved into the room, Andres had put an arm around her shoulders. The gesture, while protective and somehow comforting, was also exciting in that it seemed to announce to everyone present that she was his woman. The fact that it was for that evening only didn't really matter, for those people who eyed her with undisguised interest didn't know that, and by the time they went in to dinner Lara had become so used to him at her side and the touch of his hand, whether beneath her elbow or on her shoulder, that even she was beginning to forget it.

There was, of course, a decidedly romantic theme to the evening, with delicacies chosen for their supposed aphrodisiac qualities and an abundance of chocolate, hearts and flowers.

Lara was well aware that she came under intense scrutiny from these people, most of whom were old friends of Andres, such as the merchant banker and his wife who seemed hell bent on finding out who her father was and what he did for a living. When Lara truthfully answered that he had been a boatbuilder, it was assumed that he had been involved in some huge shipping conglomerate. This naturally led on to talk of yachts and where different guests had theirs berthed for the winter. Someone asked Lara where her family lived, and when she mentioned the boatyard and the cottage on the South Coast she was met with blank looks and the talk turned abruptly to Cowes and the Americas Cup.

Then there was the captain of industry whose main interest in life appeared to be playing polo and who asked Lara if she enjoyed the game. While she was thinking of a way to tell him that she'd never actually been to a match in her life, he went one stage further and asked her if she'd seen Andres play.

'I haven't yet had that honour,' she replied.

'Why, the man could have been a professional if he hadn't gone into medicine.'

'So where did you meet Andres?' asked a woman in a silver sequinned dress, her black hair cut into a severe geometrical shape. One of those moments of silence followed her question, the sort of lull in any conversation that occurred naturally, but which on this occa sion prompted everyone to remain silent in order to hear Lara's reply.

This time, however, it was Theo who answered, Theo, the perfect host who would not allow any guest under his roof to be embarrassed. 'Lara is a colleague,' he said lightly. 'That is where Andres and I both met her.'

There was renewed interest as people turned to look at Lara, then mercifully the moment passed as the conversation commenced once more.

When dinner was over, coffee was served in the drawing room where Lara found herself on a window-seat that overlooked the street. On the far side of the room she saw that Andres had been waylaid by a group of people who seemed to have trapped him in a corner, and as she leaned forward to stir her coffee, Annabel joined her and her heart sank. She had been on the point of congratulating herself on how well the evening was going, but she knew that Annabel could prove to be the toughest challenge yet to the deception being played out by herself and Andres.

'Lara, at last, time for a little chat,' said Annabel as she sat down and flicked back her sleek blonde hair. 'Tell me, darling, are you enjoying yourself?'

'Oh, yes, very much, thank you.' Lara smiled brightly in an attempt to hide her sudden nervousness. 'You have a beautiful home.'

'Why, thank you. I must say, Theo and I really do love it here.'

'Do you have children?' asked Lara, desperate to draw the conversation away from herself and Andres.

'Yes, we have two,' Annabel replied. 'William who is eight and Felicity who is three.'

'How lovely,' murmured Lara.

'We were so thrilled when Andres said he wanted to bring you tonight.' Annabel, it seemed, had no intention of talking about herself or her children. 'He's been on his own for far too long.' She narrowed her eyes slightly. 'You do know about Consuela?'

'Yes, of course,' Lara replied, thankful that Andres had put her in the picture.

'We feared for him, you know.' Annabel lowered her voice and out of the corner of her eye Lara saw the slightly anxious expression on Andres's face as he looked towards them. 'At the time of her death and since…'

'Since?' Lara tried to appear interested.

'Yes. He hasn't seemed to be able to get over her death.'

'It takes some people longer than others.' Swiftly Lara came to his defence.

'Well, yes, I know.' Annabel seemed a little taken aback and Lara got the impression she was the type of woman who was used to her friends agreeing with everything she said. 'But five years is a long time, you have to admit—we really were worried about him. We've tried, heaven knows we've tried, to introduce him to the right sort of women…'

'What do you mean, the right sort of women?' asked Lara in feigned innocence.

'Well—women like yourself, well bred, from the right sort of background, with the right connections…'

'And none of these women matched up to what Andres wanted?' Still the innocent look, but Annabel was frowning now.

'No…but we were prepared to keep trying. But all that's unnecessary now because he has you…' She paused. 'So tell me,' she went on after a moment, 'you are a colleague of Andres and Theo?'

'Yes,' Lara replied, 'I'm a nurse at the Roseberry and I also work on a burns unit at the hospital in Surrey where Andres is doing locum work.'

'Really?' Annabel sounded surprised and Lara suppressed a smile, certain now that Annabel had decided that she was if not a fellow consultant to Andres and Theo then at least a doctor.

'And your home—is that also in Surrey, or do you live here in town?' she added almost hopefully.

'I live with my sister and her children,' Lara replied simply.

'Really?' Annabel didn't have to pretend surprise this time. 'Your sister...?'

'Yes, she was involved in an accident where she was badly burned and her vision was impaired. Shortly after that her husband left her and their three children. I moved in to help out.'

'That's...amazing.' Annabel stared at her and Lara had the distinct impression she was lost for words, that what she had just told her bore no resemblance to what she'd been expecting to hear or what she would have deemed appropriate for a partner for Andres. Thankfully, at that moment Andres extricated himself from the group that surrounded him and made his way across to the window-seat, where he sat down beside Lara.

'Andres, darling.' Annabel still looked faintly bemused. 'Lara was just telling me all about herself.'

'Is that so?' Andres turned to Lara and as he did so he lifted his hand and, slipping it beneath her hair, gently stroked the back of her neck.

The unexpectedness of the gesture electrified her,

sending shivers up and down her spine, rendering her speechless.

It was Annabel who answered. 'Yes,' she said. 'She was telling me about her sister and how she moved in with her and her children. I think that's amazing.'

'I think,' said Andres as he continued to caress the nape of Lara's neck, 'that you will find that Lara is a pretty amazing sort of person.'

'I'm beginning to realise that.' Annabel gave a short laugh then, rising to her feet, she said, 'We will shortly be moving on to this Valentine's do at the club. I hope you two are still up for it?'

'Of course,' Andres replied smoothly. 'Why wouldn't we be?'

'I'm not what they expected,' said Lara softly, as Annabel moved away.

'So what?' His gaze met hers and once again the shivers coursed up and down her spine. 'You are everything I expected.'

She wasn't certain quite what he meant. She only knew she was quite content to go along with the party as in a series of black cabs they moved from Chelsea to the club in the West End that was holding the Valentine's party.

The interior of the club was seductively lit and decorated with heart-shaped balloons, streamers and strategically placed plaster Cupids. A live band played appropriate music and entwined couples swayed gently on the dance floor. They sat in a velvet-draped alcove together with Theo and Annabel and several others, and still the champagne flowed as ties were loosened and discarded and collars unbuttoned. Lara knew that sooner or later Andres would ask her to dance, that it would be expected of them, and sure enough the moment came when he rose to his feet and, turning to her, stretched out his hand. He took hers, drew her to her feet and led her onto the floor.

'They are all watching us,' she murmured as he drew her into his arms.

'They will,' he murmured back. 'Better not disappoint them, then.'

It felt good in his arms, right somehow, as if it was where she was meant to be. Slowly they moved among the other couples swaying to the sensual rhythm. He held her close, so close that she could feel the beating of his heart and, with his head lowered, his cheek through her hair. They stayed like that, on the floor, content to be alone in the crowd for a long time, so long, in fact, that Lara had to remind herself that this was purely pretence, that none of it was real. But when Andres made a whispered request that she put her arms around his neck she was only too happy to oblige.

And for Lara, at least, the evening was over too soon and the moment came when they spilled out of the club in the early hours covered in coloured streamers and once again black cabs were hailed. This was the moment when Lara imagined Andres would arrange for a cab to take her home, but somehow they found themselves sharing with Theo and Annabel.

'We'll drop you off first,' Theo said as they took their seats. A little later, when they reached Andres's home and found themselves on the pavement, Lara realised that his friends had automatically assumed they would be spending the night together.

'Sorry about this,' muttered Andres as he unlocked his front door and Theo and Annabel waved from the rear window of the taxi.

'It's all right,' said Lara, sad now that the wonderful evening was over.

'Come and have a nightcap,' he said, leading the way through the hall and into the drawing room. He brought coffee and brandy and they sat on the sofa and talked.

'I want to thank you,' he said. 'The evening was a great success.'

'You think we fooled them?' Lara threw him a sidelong glance.

He hesitated before answering. 'I wouldn't really like to call it that,' he said at last.

'But that is what we did, isn't it?' she asked. 'Wasn't that the whole point of the exercise, to take me so that they wouldn't arrange anyone else for you and presumably to make them believe that you and I are in a relationship…or at the very least to bring home to them the fact that you are perfectly capable of, well, of moving on and of arranging your own affairs?'

'Ye-e-es…' he agreed slowly, but Lara thought he sounded uneasy. 'The thing is,' he went on after a moment, 'I've enjoyed the evening immensely…'

'You sound as if you didn't expect to.' She allowed a teasing note to enter her voice.

'Well, in the past these things have been a strain. I think I told you…'

'Yes,' she agreed, 'you did. But this time was different—is that what you're saying?'

He nodded. 'Yes,' he admitted, 'this time was different. I enjoyed it, and that's something that hasn't happened for…well, for a very long time.'

She knew he meant since Consuela had died but he didn't say that. Instead, he stretched out his long legs and with his arms along the top of the sofa he rested his head on the cushion and briefly closed his eyes. It was the most relaxed Lara had ever seen him, and as she studied the lean lines of his profile her heart went out to him. Then quite suddenly he opened his eyes and turned his head to look at her. 'Was it awful for you?'

She frowned. 'What do you mean?' she asked.

'Well, they were so nosy, wanting to know all about you and your family.'

'Didn't you think they would be?' Again she was gently teasing. 'They care about you, Andres—they want to see you happy again.'

'Yes,' he agreed, 'I know, but they can be rather overbearing, Annabel especially. She was quizzing you about Cassie, wasn't she?'

'Not really quizzing. She wanted to know where I lived so I told her about Cassie and the children.'

'And at dinner all those questions about your parents and your family background—I'm sorry, Lara, I should have guessed it would be like that. I should never have put you through it…' He ran one hand over his head, the gesture somehow both apologetic and embarrassed.

'It's all right,' she said gently, 'really it is. I may not have given them the answers they quite wanted to hear, like the fact that my father worked in a small family-owned boatyard and wasn't some shipping tycoon…'

'Oh, God, were they that bad?' He stared at her, appalled. 'Oh, Lara, I am sorry.'

'Don't worry about it.'

'But I do. I would never have you humiliated for the world. I suppose now you would never consider repeating the event?'

'Repeating the event?' She stared at him, wondering if he meant purely to fool his friends again. 'I'm not sure we could keep up the pretence for too long. I'm sure someone would suspect, probably Annabel.'

'I wasn't meaning keeping up any pretence,' he said softly. 'I was thinking more about you and I getting to know one another properly.'

She stared at him, hardly able to believe what she was hearing, then, as an expression of pure tenderness came into his eyes, she felt her pulse begin to race.

'Would you like that, Lara?' he asked softly. Reaching out his hand, he gently touched her cheek.

'Yes,' she whispered, 'yes, Andres, I would.' She felt a little surge of pleasure at his words but something deep inside her urged caution. This man was still on the rebound from his wife, and she had her own obligations. 'I realise you're not looking to replace Consuela,' she said at last, 'and that's fine because my first commitment is to Cassie. So, yes, I would like to see you again but don't worry that I'll want more than you are able to give.'

He was quiet for a long moment, as if considering what she had just said, then he looked at his watch. 'It's late,' he said, 'very late—too late, I think, to call a cab to take you all the way back to Byfield. I think you should stay here for what is left of the night.'

She stared at him, not actually certain what he meant. Did he mean that they should spend the rest of the night together? Quite suddenly she was reminded of Sue and the comments she had made, implying that Andres would want repayment for arranging the job at the Roseberry for her. For a moment her blood ran cold. Was this what it had all been about? Had it all been a ruse to get her into bed with him?

'You could stay in the room you used earlier,' he said, his words explaining exactly what he meant.

'Yes.' A wave of relief swept over her, relief that there was no subterfuge, no trickery. 'Yes, that makes sense—as you say, it is very late.'

'Will Cassie be worried about you?' he asked, and she was touched by his concern.

'She will have gone to sleep but she may be concerned in the morning if she finds I haven't come home, so I'll leave a message on her answering-machine, telling her not to worry.' She stood up and Andres also hauled himself to his feet and stood for a moment looking down at her, his expression somehow unreadable.

'Thank you, Lara,' he said at last. 'For everything.' Gently he put his arms around her and dropped the lightest of kisses on her forehead.

Lara froze, uncertain how to respond, wondering whether if at this point she showed any form of encouragement, it would indicate that she would be happy to spend the night in his bed. And was she, now that she knew there was no trickery on his part? Would she want that to happen? Part of her screamed, yes, that was exactly what she wanted, that she had been attracted to this devastatingly handsome man from the very moment that she'd set eyes on him, but the more sensible side of her urged caution, extreme caution. By his own admission he wasn't yet over his wife, wasn't ready for another relationship, and even though he had just expressed a desire to get to know her better, that did not necessarily mean he was ready to embark upon a full-scale affair. For Lara an affair, which included a sexual relationship, needed a high level of commitment, something which she very much doubted Andres was prepared to offer. She had learnt a harsh lesson with Sven, for he had been unable to offer much in the way of commitment and she had been hurt when he had left.

'Goodnight, Lara,' he said softly, making any decision on her part unnecessary.

'Goodnight, Andres,' she replied.

## CHAPTER NINE

HE COULDN'T believe how he felt. All he knew was that he hadn't felt this way in a very long time. He lay on his bed, his hands behind his head, totally unable to sleep, knowing that Lara was in a room only yards away from his own. He was amazed that the evening had been the success it had been. His friends, mainly Annabel, had quizzed Lara as much, if not more, than he had thought they would, but Lara herself hadn't seemed to mind that, had even made excuses for them, saying that it was understandable and that they were only concerned for him. They had liked her, he was sure of that. He knew them all well enough to be able to gauge their reactions and he was confident that they approved of Lara—not that that should make the slightest difference. The object of the exercise hadn't been whether or not they approved of Lara—it had quite simply been to stop them matchmaking.

He hoped Lara had enjoyed herself. He was pretty sure she had. He knew, somewhat surprisingly, that he had. It had started almost from the moment she had appeared, descending the stairway. He had been standing in the hall and as he had looked up the sight of her had almost taken his breath away. She'd looked absolutely stunning in a black dress that had revealed the creamy skin of her neck and shoulders and the soft curve of her breasts, while that wild, fiery mane of her hair had been loose, framing her face seductively.

When they had reached Theo's and Annabel's he

had seen the admiration in the eyes of the other men when they had first set eyes on Lara, and it had boosted his ego to know that she had been with him. He had worried about her at dinner, especially when she hadn't been seated near him, but she had seemed to take everything in her stride, including the relentless questioning about herself and her family. And later, when Annabel had trapped her in the window-seat, she hadn't seemed fazed by the older woman's interrogation.

But it had been after that, at the club, when the flame of something unbelievable had been ignited deep inside him. It had happened when he had taken her onto the floor to dance and she had seemed to melt in his arms. He had held her close, unable to believe the explosion of emotion that had gone on inside him. He had wanted her, there had been no denying the clamouring or demands of his body, and later when, once again, briefly, he had held her and gently kissed her forehead, he could have sworn that, unbelievably, there was a chance she might feel the same way.

But supposing he had attempted to take things further. Supposing he had made love to her and even now she was lying beside him? If that had happened, she would think that had been his intention all along, that he'd had an ulterior motive for inviting her to the party. And deep down Andres knew that was not the case. Oh, he wanted her right enough, just as there had been others he'd wanted since Consuela's death, but they had been brief, momentary affairs, a slaking of lust, while this, with Lara, he knew was neither. This was more, much, much more. This was a reawakening of a feeling he thought had died with Consuela, but even more than that, this held some other emotion, something he was at a loss to define. There was a sense of excitement, of discovery, of the unknown—something, he realised in amazement, that had been missing with Consuela, maybe because they had always known one another and there had been no real voyage of discovery. But with Lara everything was different. Lara was new, unknown and full of exciting possibilities. But was he ready for that? Did he really want to embark on such a relationship?

And what of Lara herself? Would she be prepared to take things further? She'd seemed pleased when he had suggested they get to know one another better, but was she merely being polite? She'd already indicated that relationships for her were difficult because of her home situation, that her sister still lacked the confidence to cope on her own. Maybe, he thought as he glanced at his bedside clock and saw that it was nearly four-thirty, it was time to put into action the plan that had been forming at the back of his mind for the last few weeks. But first he really would have to try to put all thoughts of Lara—and the fact that she was sleeping in his house—right out of his mind and try and snatch a few hours' sleep himself.

When she awoke to the early morning sunshine that streamed through the bedroom window, Lara couldn't for a moment remember where she was. Then it all came flooding back. The evening at the McFarlanes', the dancing at the club and returning to Andres's beautiful home, where it had been decided she should stay the night.

Just for one moment, when he had held her briefly and kissed her before wishing her goodnight, she had thought he'd been about to suggest they sleep together. At that moment she had wanted him, wanted him badly, and if he had so much as indicated that was what he'd wanted, she probably would have agreed. That she would, no doubt, have regretted it was something else entirely. With a deep sigh she turned onto her back. Maybe she should simply have thrown caution to the winds—let him know that was what she wanted. At least that way she would have spent one night with him and by now would know what it was like to have him make love to her. Now she would probably never know, for their little arrangement was over and was never likely to be repeated. He had suggested they get to know one another better and although she had agreed, her pulse quickening even at the thought, she now wondered if he'd simply said that on the spur of the moment and was now regretting it.

Half an hour later, after she'd showered and dressed, she joined Andres downstairs in the kitchen where he was preparing the most delicious-smelling coffee, together with rounds of hot buttered toast and chilled orange juice.

'Hello,' she said, almost shyly, when he looked up as she entered the room.

'Lara.' Did his expression soften, take on a tender look, or did she imagine it? 'I hope you slept well?'

'Oh, yes,' she replied. 'Thank you.' It was a lie and she knew it, because she had spent most of what had been left of the night just lying there, thinking of him and of how he was so close to her yet so far. 'And you?' she asked after a moment. 'Did you sleep well?'

'Yes. I crashed out as soon as my head touched the pillow.'

'Oh, good,' she said, her heart sinking as she realised he hadn't been affected as she had. But, then, why should he be? After all, he had made it perfectly plain why he had asked her to do what he had, and he'd not given any indication that he wanted to take things much further. It was true he'd danced with her, held her close, even kissed her, albeit lightly, but wouldn't he have behaved that way with any woman? Why should it be any different with her? And wasn't the whole point of this exercise that he didn't want to be involved with anyone—that he wasn't ready, that he merely wanted his friends to stop their meddling? 'There wasn't too much of the night left,' she said now, in an attempt to keep the conversation light and non-committal.

'You're right,' he agreed as he poured orange juice for her and indicated for her to take a seat at the large, central table. 'We talked longer than I thought, but somehow there seemed to be rather a lot to say.' He paused and took a seat opposite her. He was dressed casually this morning in T-shirt and jeans, more casual than she'd ever seen him, and, she was forced to admit, he looked even more handsome. She, of course, only had the clothes she'd worn for work the previous day, not imagining she would be staying overnight.

'I'm glad it's Saturday and we're both off duty,' he said, taking a mouthful of his juice. 'At least we can take our time. Did you phone Cassie?' he asked suddenly.

'I left a message, telling her not to worry,' Lara replied, sipping her own juice and thinking how delicious it tasted.

'And would she have worried?'

'If she'd woken up and found I hadn't come home, you mean?'

He nodded.

'Yes, she'd probably have had me dead in a ditch somewhere.'

'Has she always been so protective of you?' he asked curiously.

'Not really.' Lara considered. 'Although I have to say,' she added after a moment, 'when we were small she always looked after me. But, no, she has only really been like this since I moved in with her.'

'So she's become very dependent on you?'

'Well, yes, I suppose she has.' Lara paused again reflectively. 'But I daresay that's understandable, given the circumstances. She completely lost her confidence, you know, especially after Dave left her and, of course, she's had depression to battle with as well…'

Andres was silent for a moment then, leaning forward and passing her the toast, he said casually, 'Actually, while we are on the subject of Cassie, there was something I wanted to put to you.'

'Oh?' She looked up, 'What is that?'

'I was wondering if she would agree to having further surgery on her face.'

She stared at him across the table, but the expression in his dark eyes was unfathomable. 'We didn't think more surgery was possible,' she said slowly at last. 'She certainly wasn't offered any more at the time.'

'I think I could improve the scarring,' he said quietly.

'But would that be available for her? And if it was, wouldn't there be a long wait?'

'I meant for her to come to the Roseberry,' he said, helping himself to marmalade, spreading it carefully on his toast with all the precision of his profession.

Lara was silent for a moment, mesmerised by his hands, then, taking a deep breath, she said, 'It's a wonderful idea, Andres, but I'm afraid it would be out of the question.'

'May I ask why?' He raised his eyebrows, the knife poised over his plate.

'I've seen the fees that are charged at the Roseberry,' she replied, 'and you have to understand there is simply no way that we could afford those.'

'That wasn't my intention,' he replied, calmly cutting his toast and setting the knife down.

'Not your intention…?' Lara frowned.

'No, Lara,' he replied firmly. 'The suggestion came from me. You are a friend—there would be no fee.'

She stared at him, hardly able to believe what she was hearing, then, as she felt the tears begin to prickle at the back of her eyes, she said, 'We couldn't possibly expect you to do that…' Her voice was husky and she was forced to clear her throat.

'But you aren't expecting me to do anything. It was my idea and if I can't do something to help a friend…' He trailed off, and shrugged.

'I don't know what to say…' The tears that had been so dangerously close spilled over now and she dashed them away with the back of her hand.

'Then don't say anything,' he said. After a moment's silence in which Lara struggled to regain her composure, he went on, 'What do you think Cassie's reaction would be?'

'I think she will be shocked and amazed, just like I was,' she said slowly, 'but once she gets over that I'm certain she will be delighted. She was always disappointed with the results of the skin grafting that was done after her accident.'

He nodded as if in agreement then said, 'Well, as I told you, I don't want to apportion blame to a fellow surgeon, and in his defence, he probably did all he could at the time—sometimes these things need to be reviewed after a period of time—but I feel quite strongly that I could bring about an improvement for her.'

'Oh, Andres.' Lara stared at him across the table, filled with emotion at his generosity. 'We would be so grateful if you could. If you could just make it a little easier for Cassie to face the world, I'm sure that would help her depression…'

'I can't, of course, do anything for her impaired vision.'

'No,' she replied. 'I realise that and I have to say she really does cope with that aspect of things very well.'

'Right.' He stood up and fetched a large coffee-pot. 'The next thing is how best to broach this to Cassie. Should I come in and see her when I take you home, or would it be best for you to approach her first and let her get used to the idea before I enter the equation?'

'I think it would be best if I talked to her first,' said Lara slowly. 'That is, if you don't mind,' she added anxiously, not wanting him to think she wasn't grateful for his kindness.

'Not at all,' he said firmly. 'This is a delicate matter and needs to be approached sensitively.'

They changed the subject after that and talked of other things—the evening they had shared and the people who had been at the Chelsea house.

'What's this about you being of professional standard at polo?' she asked as they lingered over their second cup of coffee, neither of them seemingly in any hurry to move, as if doing so would somehow break the spell that had been woven the night before.

'Whoever told you that?' He gave a short laugh.

'Now, let me see,' Lara mused. 'Was it the merchant banker or was it the chief executive of that well-known oil company?'

Andres pulled a face, knowing she was teasing him over the status enjoyed by his friends. 'Well, whoever it was,' he said, 'they need to get their facts right.'

'But you do play polo?' she persisted.

'Yes,' he admitted, 'I do, but I'm hardly professional standard.'

'You must be good, though, for him to say that.'

'Maybe.' He shrugged. 'But what you have to remember is that where I come from we practically lived in the saddle. I was put up onto a horse almost before I could walk. When I was a boy I used to ride out across the pampas every day.'

'It sounds wonderful,' she said with a little sigh, then after a moment she added, 'Cassie and I used to ride.'

'Really?' His interest was undeniable.

'There were stables near where we lived. My parents couldn't afford lessons so Cassie and I used to help with the mucking out and grooming and in return they allowed us to help exercise the horses. We soon learnt how to ride—we used to take the horses on the beach or for long gallops across the downs.'

'It sounds as if you enjoyed it,' he said with a smile.

'Oh, we did,' she replied passionately. 'It was wonderful—there's nothing quite like cantering through the surf at the water's edge and feeling the salt air on your face.'

'Unless it's a day spent in the high sierras, with golden eagles circling above in an unbelievably blue sky,' he said lightly. As Lara was imagining the picture he had just painted, he said, 'Do you still ride?'

'Unfortunately, no.' She shook her head. 'There never seems to be the time or the opportunity these days, and since Cassie's accident…' She trailed off but her meaning was clear.

'Maybe we should create both,' he said. 'The time and the opportunity. Maybe we should go together to do something we both obviously enjoy.'

'Do you mean that?' She stared at him.

'Of course I do. I'll find a suitable stable and organise something.'

'That would be wonderful,' she said, hardly able to take in the things that this man was about to make happen—first, another operation to make life more bearable for Cassie and then, for her, the possibility of a return to a long-held passion.

'More coffee?' He held up the pot.

'Just a little,' she replied, adding reluctantly, 'Then I really will have to think about going.'

It was late morning by the time they got back to Byfield. Andres brought the car to a halt in a space a few yards from the house and switched off the engine.

'Are you sure you wouldn't like me to come and talk to Cassie now?' he asked, resting his hands on the steering-wheel and turning his head to look at her.

'No,' she said. 'If you don't mind, Andres, I think we'll leave things as we said. I still think I need to pick my moment with Cassie. She's not too good with shocks or anything unexpected these days. But you're very welcome to come in for a drink or something,' she added hurriedly.

'No.' He glanced at his watch. 'If you don't mind, I think I'll head back into town—I have things I need to do.'

'Of course,' she murmured. 'Well, thank you for bringing me home.'

'Lara, it was the least I could do. And it's me who should be thanking you for coming with me last night. I really do appreciate it, you know.'

'Don't mention it.' She smiled. 'I enjoyed it.'

'Goodbye, Lara.' Gently he touched her hand and for a moment her skin tingled.

'Bye, Andres.' Turning away from him, she fumbled with the door catch and in her confusion almost tumbled out of the car onto the pavement.

'See you on Monday at St Joseph's,' he said as she leaned forward and looked into the car before closing the door, her gaze meeting and holding his.

'Yes,' she agreed, 'see you on Monday.'

And then he was gone and she was left on the pavement, staring at the rear of his car as it disappeared down the road and turned the corner at the end. With a little shiver she pulled her coat around her, turning up the collar against the chill of the February wind, then slowly she walked up to the house and fitted her key into the lock.

It was while she was taking her coat off in the hall that it struck her how quiet the house was. Usually on a Saturday morning evidence of three lively children was everywhere, from music from their CD players to noise from the television or the sound of a football being kicked against the wall outside in the back yard. She lifted her head and listened, but there was no sound. Thinking the children must be out, she made her way to the family room at the rear of the house where she guessed Cassie would be. She pushed open the door and was astonished to find Luke and Sophie sitting in silence at the kitchen table, while in the far corner Cassie was sitting in her armchair with Callum on her lap.

'Cassie?' Lara froze in the doorway, sensing something was not as it should be. 'What is it? What's wrong?'

Neither Cassie nor the children spoke, but Cassie's gaze moved from Lara to a point behind the door.

With a frown Lara looked around the door where to her further amazement she found her brother-in-law, Dave, seated in a chair.

'What in the world did you say?' It was Monday morning at St Joseph's and Lara had just told Katie how she had found Dave sitting in the kitchen.

'I really didn't know quite what to say,' Lara admitted. 'The children seemed subdued and a little shell-shocked, and Cassie—well, I wasn't sure how she felt about having him turn up like that out of the blue.'

'What did he want? Surely he's not expecting her to take him back after walking out on her the way he did?'

'Actually, yes, that's exactly want he does want.'

'And what does Cassie think about that?' Katie looked astounded.

'It's hard to say really,' Lara replied. 'All along she'd said she could never forgive him for what he did, but just recently her attitude towards him seems to have softened a little.'

'Does he have a job?'

'Apparently so—at his old firm, actually, as a software technician.'

'And where is he living?'

'He's renting a flat on the other side of Byfield. Callum had already said he'd seen him in town and outside his school. We weren't sure whether or not to believe him at first—we thought perhaps it was just wishful thinking on his part.'

'Poor little boy,' said Katie.

'Yes,' Lara agreed, 'but it looks like he was right all along.'

'How do you think the children will feel if their father does come home?'

'Well, Sophie is ecstatic at the idea and Callum, of course, but I'm not sure about Luke. I think Dave will have some hard work convincing Luke that he really means this—that's always supposing, of course, that Cassie does take him back.'

'And what about you?' Katie's eyes narrowed.

'What do you mean, what about me?' asked Lara lightly.

'Well, if Dave and Cassie start playing happy families again, where would that leave you? I seem to remember there not being a lot of space in that little house.'

'You're right. There isn't.' Lara pulled a face. 'Cassie has assured me there's a home there for me whatever happens, but if they do get back together, I would look for somewhere else.'

'Talking of you,' said Katie as she smoothed down her uniform and straightened her belt, 'how did the Valentine's party go? I was dying to know but what with you telling me all this about Dave and Cassie, it went right out of my head.'

'It went very well, actually,' Lara replied.

Katie stared at her. 'Go on, tell me about it,' she urged.

'I'm not sure we have time now.' Lara glanced at her watch.

'We've got five minutes,' Katie protested. 'Go on, I

can't wait till our break. Reverend Sister will just have to wait.'

'OK.' Lara laughed at her friend's eagerness. 'Well, you know it was at Andres's friends' home in Chelsea?'

'Yes. What was the house like?'

'Very grand, but lovely as well. We had drinks first, then a dinner party for twelve and after that we all went on to a club where there was a huge party going on.'

'Was there dancing?' asked Katie.

'Oh, yes.' Lara's tone softened as she recalled that particular aspect of the evening and remembered anew how it had felt to be in Andres's arms.

'And did he dance with you—Andres?'

'Yes, of course he did. I was his date for the evening, remember.'

'Yes, I know.' Katie sounded impatient now. 'But what was he like? You know…'

'Fine.' Lara tried hard to sound casual. 'He's a very nice man.'

'Is that all?' Katie looked and sounded so disappointed it was almost comical.

'Well, what did you expect? I told you it was simply an arrangement to stop his friends lining up someone for him again.'

'Yes, I know, but I thought…I hoped…'

'I know exactly what you were hoping,' said Lara with a short laugh. 'I'm sorry to disappoint you.'

'Hang on a minute.' Katie, it seemed, was not to be deterred by this explanation. 'What happened afterwards?'

'What do you mean—afterwards?' Lara frowned. Maybe she wasn't going to get away with this as easily as she had thought.

'After you left the club, where did you go then? Did you come straight home or…or…?'

'Or what?' Lara asked coolly.

'Or did you go back to his place first?'

'Actually, yes, we did. Andres suggested a night-cap…'

'Oh, yes.' Katie was beginning to sound interested again. 'And what is his place like?'

'That, too, is very grand—a town house in Knightsbridge in one of those lovely secluded little squares.'

'Sounds rather yummy. Did he take you home or did he call a cab? Lara?' Katie persisted, when Lara remained silent.

'What?' Lara looked up at last, her expression deliberately vague.

'I said did he take you home or did—?' Katie broke off suddenly in mid-sentence and stared at Lara.

'What?' said Lara again.

'You didn't go home, did you?' Katie's voice had taken on a rather hysterical note.

Lara took a deep breath. 'Actually, no, I didn't.'

'Oh, boy!' said Katie.

'And you needn't go reading anything into that,' said Lara firmly, 'because absolutely nothing happened.'

'Yeah, right.'

'Katie, it didn't,' Lara protested. 'You have to believe me. Because it was so late Andres asked me if I would like to stay. I agreed and there were no strings attached. I slept in the room I had used the previous evening to get changed in…'

'And where did Andres sleep?'

'In his own room, of course.' Lara was beginning to feel exasperated with Katie. 'Where do you think?'

'I don't quite know what to think.'

'Honestly, Katie, what do you take me for?' protested Lara.

'To be perfectly honest with you,' said Katie candidly, 'I really wouldn't have blamed you if you had slept with him.'

'Katie!' Lara stared at her in mock outrage.

'Well, I wouldn't. Let's face it, he's drop-dead gorgeous—just give me half a chance, that's what I say.'

'Oh, no, not you as well,' said Lara, rolling her eyes. 'I thought it was bad enough with Sue.'

'Yeah, well, you can't blame us, and you have to admit he really is a cut above the average locum we get here, now, isn't he?'

'Yes, now you put it like that, I suppose he is,' Lara admitted. 'Listen,' she added urgently, 'we really should be getting onto the ward.'

'Yes, all right, but what I want to know is what happens now?' asked Katie curiously.

Lara had moved to the door but she paused with one hand on the handle and turned back to Katie again. 'What do you mean, what happens now?'

'Does he want to see you again? Has he asked you out?'

'I told you, it was an arrangement, a one-off.'

'OK, but that doesn't necessarily mean he can't ask you out again, does it?'

'No,' Lara agreed, 'I suppose not.'

'So has he, then?' Katie persisted.

'Not…exactly.' Lara hedged.

'What then?'

'He's going to suss out a stables so that we can go riding together, but—'

'Hah!' said Katie with obvious satisfaction. 'Now we're getting somewhere.'

'For goodness' sake,' Lara protested as they moved out into the corridor. 'Don't go reading more into that than there is. It only came up because someone said something about Andres playing polo, and later when we were talking I happened to mention that I used to enjoy horse riding... What?' she demanded, throwing Katie a sidelong glance and catching sight of her expression. 'Why are you laughing?'

'I'm sorry.' Katie chuckled. 'I can't help it. All this talk of houses in Chelsea and Knightsbridge, private clinics, fast cars, polo...'

'I know,' said Lara soberly. 'It really isn't me at all, is it?'

'Oh, it could be,' said Katie. 'Quite easily, in fact.'

Even Lara was laughing by the time they reached the ward, but she was soon obliged to put all thoughts of Andres to the back of her mind as the demands of the busy unit claimed her once more. She and Katie prepared Mary Taylor for the first of her skin grafts.

As she worked she was aware of a heightened sense of anticipation, of excitement almost, and deep in her heart she knew it was at the thought of seeing Andres again in what would be their first encounter since he had brought her home on Saturday morning. It happened just before Mary was ready to go down to Theatre, when Andres came onto the ward to see her and the other patients who were scheduled for surgery that day. As he entered the unit his dark gaze searched for Lara, found her immediately, met her own gaze and held it, both of them oblivious to those around them, momentarily in a world of their own.

When at last he was forced to look away, Lara also

turned away, only to find herself meeting Katie's questioning gaze—Katie, who quite obviously had witnessed the interchange between herself and Andres and was even now applying her own interpretation. And as Lara moved away towards the nurses' station Katie, in a passing murmur, said, 'Don't ever try to pretend to me again that there's nothing going on between you two because I'll never believe you—not in a million years would I believe you.'

'But there isn't,' whispered Lara, as Sue hurried out of her office to greet Andres.

'Maybe not yet,' muttered Katie, 'but it sure as hell is going to happen, and when it does...' she chuckled '...our Reverend Sister is going to have her nose put well and truly out of joint.'

# CHAPTER TEN

'CASSIE.' It was a few days later and Lara had picked a moment to talk to her sister when the children were in bed and the house was quiet.

'Yes?' Cassie looked up from the television where one of her favourite programmes had just finished and the credits were beginning to roll.

'We need to talk,' said Lara, coming right into the room and sitting down beside Cassie, who pressed the button of the remote control, switching off the television.

Cassie searched Lara's features, as if trying to read her sister's concerns. 'You're worried about Dave coming back,' she said at last, then, not giving Lara a chance to deny it, she carried straight on, 'Well, you needn't be. Dave and I have talked at length about this, and if and when he moves back here we are totally agreed that there is still a home here for you. We both feel that what you have done for this family is way above the call of duty…' She trailed off as Lara held up her hands.

'Whoa, Cassie, please, stop right there,' she said. 'There's something we need to get straight—there *is* something I want to discuss with you, but it isn't that.'

'No?' Cassie looked bewildered. 'It isn't?'

'No.' Lara shook her head. 'But now that you've mentioned it I may as well tell you—if you and Dave get back together, I have already made up my mind that I'll be moving out.'

'Lara—no!' Cassie protested.

'Yes, Cassie,' she replied firmly. 'If all of you are living together again as a family, there's no room here for a permanent house guest.'

'But we couldn't let you just go,' protested Cassie. 'Not after all your kindness. Besides, where would you go?'

'I would find myself a flat.' Lara shrugged. 'Just the same as I had before I came here. Honestly, Cassie, it wouldn't be a problem, and if it does happen I will be delighted for you and for the children. Now, to get on to what I wanted to talk about—and, actually, this also concerns you and your future.'

'Me?' Cassie looked startled and unconsciously her hand flew to her face, her fingers gently tracing the lines of scarring.

'Yes.' Lara nodded. 'You and Andres Ricardo.'

'Me and…?' Cassie's eyes widened. 'What on earth do you mean?'

'Andres has made an incredible offer,' said Lara.

'What sort of offer?' Cassie frowned.

'He has offered to perform further surgery on your face,' said Lara gently, her voice softening as she recalled Andres's exact words.

'Further surgery?' Cassie repeated. 'I don't understand.' She shook her head in bewilderment. 'I thought…I was told at the time that was all they could do.'

'Yes,' Lara agreed, 'and at the time that was probably the case, but after seeing you Andres feels that he could improve on what was done. What do you think? Would you be willing to give it a try?' There was silence in the room, broken only by the faint whirring of the dishwasher in the kitchen.

'I don't know, Lara…I really don't know.' Cassie looked troubled. 'The thought of more surgery fills me with dread and…then afterwards…well, there's no guarantee it will be any better, is there?'

'I don't think Andres would have suggested it if he didn't think there was a good chance he could improve things for you.' Lara paused. 'He's good, Cassie, very good. I've seen the results of his work.'

'So where would he do this?' Cassie still sounded far from convinced, but Lara noticed that a new note had entered her voice, a note of anticipation. 'At St Joseph's?'

'No, not at St Joseph's,' Lara replied quietly. 'At the Roseberry Clinic.'

'But don't they charge the earth?' Cassie stared at her. 'We could never afford anything like that, Lara. Even if Dave comes back, I don't think there's any way we could raise that sort of money.'

'I know,' Lara replied, 'and I told Andres so, but he explained that wasn't what he intended. He said there would be no fee.'

'No fee?' Cassie's eyes widened again.

'That's what he said—that he had offered to do this, that we hadn't asked and that he was offering it as a friend.'

'Oh, Lara.' There were tears in Cassie's eyes now. 'I don't know what to say.'

'Think about it. Sleep on it before you make any decision,' said Lara.

'But how kind of him…'

'He's that sort of man,' said Lara, and suddenly her own voice was husky. She realised her sister was staring at her intently.

'Lara,' Cassie began hesitantly, 'is there any chance that you and he…?'

'I don't know, Cassie—really, I don't.'

'But you do like him?' Cassie persisted.

'Oh, yes, I like him well enough,' Lara admitted. 'I also find him very attractive, but I'm not certain anything will come of it. You see, it's like I told you before. I'm really not sure he is sufficiently over the death of his wife yet, certainly not enough for him to be thinking about starting a new relationship.'

'Five years is a long time,' said Cassie slowly.

'Yes, I know,' Lara agreed, 'but I guess it takes some people longer than others to get over something like that. Andres told me that he didn't want any sort of involvement and that was why he asked me to accompany him to the party. I've no reason to believe that since then anything has changed.'

'Well, you never know,' said Cassie hopefully. 'He may just have realised what he's been missing.'

'Like Dave, you mean?' Lara raised a questioning eyebrow.

'Yes, in a way, I suppose,' Cassie agreed.

'Do you think it's going to work out with Dave, or is it too soon to tell?'

'I think it might,' said Cassie slowly. 'He's beside himself with remorse and is begging my forgiveness…'

'And how do you feel about that?' asked Lara.

'I'm not sure yet. Most of the time I'm still as angry as hell with him…'

'And the rest of the time?'

'I guess I still love the brute,' Cassie admitted with a wry smile.

'What about the children? How do they feel about him coming home?'

'Sophie and Callum can't wait to have him back,' said Cassie slowly, 'but that's what you'd expect.'

'And Luke?'

'Oh, I think Luke more than anyone,' she replied softly.

Two days later, during a break in a shift at the Roseberry, Lara found the opportunity to speak to Andres. She met him in the corridor where the surgeons had their consulting rooms, and as he walked towards her she felt her heart leap.

'Andres,' she said, and knew she sounded breathless. 'May I have a word about Cassie?'

'Of course,' he said. 'Come in here.' He opened the door of his consulting room then stood back for her to precede him into the room. As she passed close to him she was briefly reminded of that other occasion when they had been as close, when he had held her in his arms on the dance floor. Then she tried desperately to dismiss that memory for that was surely all it was—a memory of something special that would never be repeated.

'Take a seat, Lara, please,' he said, closing the door. As she sat down he seated himself at his desk. If she hadn't known better, she would have sworn that he seemed nervous. But that was ridiculous. Why should a man like Andres Ricardo, a highly successful consultant, be nervous in the presence of a member of his own staff?

'You've spoken to Cassie about my offer?' he asked at last.

'Yes,' she replied, 'I have.'

'And what was her reaction?'

'Well, she was pretty stunned at first.' She glanced

up. 'Oh, don't get me wrong. She was overwhelmed by your generosity, but...'

'She was also apprehensive at the thought of more surgery with no guarantee of improvement—that is perfectly understandable.'

'Yes, I know,' said Lara quickly, 'so I urged her to sleep on it, to think about it, which she did...'

'And?' he said softly.

'And she has said she would be delighted to accept your offer.'

'Good,' he said briskly. 'I'll fit her into my schedule at the very first opportunity. I can't make too many promises but I feel sure that what I am able to do will give Cassie more confidence to face the world.'

'Speaking of that,' said Lara, 'something else has happened that could make a big difference. Her husband Dave is on the scene again—he wants her to take him back.'

'And how does Cassie feel about that?' asked Andres.

'Oh, she'll forgive him—there's little doubt about that.'

'And where would that leave you?' His gaze met hers across the desk.

'I would find a flat and move out,' she said with a little shrug.

'So you would have your life back?' he said softly.

She smiled. 'Yes, I suppose you could say that.'

There was silence for a moment, a silence that somehow, poignantly, seemed to signify the end of one era and at the same time herald the start of another.

'I've been doing a little homework,' he said at last, breaking the silence.

'What sort of homework?' She was aware that her pulse had started to race.

'I've found some riding stables,' he said. 'They're near Godalming and I think they are exactly what we want—I looked them over and the horses are in excellent shape. Are you still keen to go?'

'Oh, yes,' she said. 'There's nothing I'd like better.'

'Are you off duty next Saturday?'

'Yes,' she replied, and her pulse was racing faster than ever. 'Yes, I am.'

'Good,' he said with a little sigh of satisfaction. 'So am I, so shall I book us in?'

'Oh, yes,' she said, 'yes, please.'

There was a severe frost on Friday night and on Saturday morning the ground was hard and a mist lingered across the Surrey countryside. Andres picked Lara up very early and his breath caught in his throat when she came out of the house dressed in riding trousers and boots, a yellow polo-necked sweater and a hacking jacket, and with her mass of hair tied back from her face with a velvet ribbon.

'You look great,' he said as she slipped into the passenger seat beside him.

'The jacket is Cassie's,' she said. 'The trousers are mine and luckily I still had my riding boots. I don't have a helmet, though,' she added.

'We can hire helmets,' he said. For some reason he was feeling nervous. He still couldn't quite believe she had agreed to come out with him, and even though this was a far from conventional date, he knew he desperately wanted it to be a success because for the first time since Consuela's death he had found a woman whom he really wanted to be with. They drove through the grey of the early morning and out into the Surrey countryside, where the bare branches of the trees were etched sharply against the pearly light of the sky. The stables were already a hive of activity in spite of the earliness of the hour as stalls were mucked out, horses groomed and the yard hosed down.

Andres was given a huge, dappled grey stallion to ride and Lara a smaller chestnut mare. 'She has the sweetest temperament,' said the groom as he led the horse out of her stall and held her head while Lara mounted.

Within half an hour they were heading out of the stableyard at a brisk trot, settling down to a canter as they reached the bridleway. The ground was hard with frost and the ice-covered puddles crackled beneath the horses' hooves while the animals' breath hung heavy in the cold morning air. It felt good to Andres to be back in the saddle again and although both the countryside and the climate were as far removed from his beloved Argentina as it was possible to be, he felt content. With the horse he was riding, the crisp English February morning and more than all of that, with the woman who rode a little ahead of him, a woman whom he was increasingly beginning to realise had the power to change his life for ever if only he would let her.

When they reached a large stretch of open common, they gave the horses their heads and settled down to an exhilarating gallop. As they rode, the pale morning sunlight finally broke through the cloud, banishing the last of the mist. They rode for miles until at last Andres, who was slightly ahead of Lara, reined in his horse and dismounted, indicating for her to do the same. Leading both horses forward to the edge of a small thicket, where catkins cascaded from the trees and drifts of snowdrops covered the ground, he tethered them securely to a branch of a tree.

He removed his helmet, seeing that Lara was doing likewise, then he walked back to her and on a sudden, uncontrollable impulse he gathered her into his arms, the gesture natural and spontaneous. For a long moment he just held her close, aware as he did so of her heart beating against his own. Then, moving slightly, he looked down into her eyes, those trusting green eyes that had fascinated him from the very moment he had first gazed into them and, he realised now, had captivated him, utterly and completely.

'Lara,' he murmured, then, unable to hold back for a second more, he took her face between his hands, his fingers becoming entangled in the tendrils of hair that had escaped from the band. He brought his mouth down onto hers, a thrill shooting through his body as her lips parted to receive him. Gently with his tongue he explored the warm, sweet softness of her mouth, eager now and encouraged by the unexpected warmth of her response as she allowed her hands to caress the back of his neck, shuddering with delight as her fingers stroked his short hair. He closed his eyes and as the scent of her filled his senses he was no longer in the crisp, chill air of a February morning but in that sun-drenched, flower-filled summer meadow that always reminded him of her. 'Lara. Oh, Lara,' he moaned softly, as at last he drew away slightly. 'If only you knew how much I've longed to do that.'

'When?' she asked teasingly. 'When did you long to do that?'

'So many times,' he replied ruefully, 'but never more than that night when I held you in my arms and we danced...'

'Why didn't you?' she asked softly.

'I thought you would think I was using you,' he admitted. 'That I'd had an ulterior motive in asking you to come to the party with me.'

'And you hadn't?' she asked innocently.

'No, of course not,' he protested. 'The reasons I asked you to come with me were perfectly genuine—I was fed up with Annabel and her matchmaking and really didn't want to become involved with anyone...'

'So what happened?' The teasing note was back in her voice again.

'You happened,' he said simply. 'I had no idea the effect you would have on me. I guess I was attracted to you from the very start but I really didn't bargain for the way I felt that night—and ever since.'

'What are you saying?' she said, gently reaching up and touching the corner of his mouth with the tips of her fingers.

'I'm not really sure,' he admitted. 'I didn't think I was ready to fall in love again...'

'And now?' she whispered, moving her fingers to trace the shape of his lips.

'I believe that is exactly what is happening.' His voice was suddenly husky and as he struggled to find the right words to explain further, Lara stood on tiptoe and, reaching up, drew him down to her again. Their kiss was longer this time, more intense, with a stirring of a passion that more than hinted of what pleasure was to come. At last, when they eventually drew apart, he once again looked searchingly into her eyes. 'But what about you, Lara?' He hardly dared to ask, afraid she would tell him this was all one-sided, that she had only gone with him in the first place to help him out and that she was only here with him now because of her love of riding. 'How do you feel?'

She considered for a moment and he held his breath. 'I feel,' she said at last, 'as if I'm on the edge of something, on the brink of some huge adventure, full of excitement. I can't remember ever feeling this way before. It's like I've been waiting for this to happen all my life and now that it is happening, I can't quite believe it.'

His heart leapt at her words. 'So this could be love?' he said softly.

'Yes,' she said slowly, 'I really think it could.' She closed her eyes as once again she lifted her face for his kiss, and behind them on the edge of the thicket one of the horses whickered softly.

The following two weeks for Lara were like nothing she had ever known before as her life began to change beyond all recognition. Her brother-in-law moved back into the family home and, as he and Cassie and their children attempted to rebuild their lives, Lara moved into a flat that had become vacant in the same building where Katie lived.

'Not that I think you'll be here for long,' said Katie with a sniff as she helped Lara carry her possessions inside.

'I can't think what you mean,' said Lara lightly.

'Oh, yes, you can,' said Katie. 'You know exactly what I mean. So does everyone else at St Joseph's. Honestly, you only have to see the way he looks at you to know what is happening. Even Sue's accepted it now,' she added with a chuckle.

'She's still a bit frosty with me,' said Lara.

'What do you expect? She's spent a fortune on updating herself and what happens? You come along and whisk away the object of her desire right from under her nose. Anyway, what's a little frost when you have a sizzling passion to keep you warm?'

'It's hardly that—yet,' Lara protested.

'You mean you haven't...?' Katie threw her an incredulous glance.

'We are taking things slowly,' said Lara, almost primly. 'You know, getting to know each other properly, that sort of thing.'

'You must be mad,' said Katie with a sigh. 'A hunk like that—I would have grabbed him at the first opportunity.'

'He isn't like that,' said Lara. 'In fact, he's quite old-fashioned. I really believe he's wooing me—you know, chocolates and flowers, candlelit dinners, things like that.'

'Sounds dreamy,' said Katie enviously. 'No one ever wooed me like that.'

'It *is* rather lovely,' Lara admitted, 'and very different. But, then, Andres is different to anyone else I've ever known.'

'You can say that again,' said Katie with a sigh. After a pause, she added, 'When is he doing Cassie's op?'

'Early next week,' Lara replied. 'He's seen her for the initial consultation and he's booked her into the Roseberry for the actual surgery.'

'Will you be on duty?' asked Katie dubiously.

'No.' Lara shook her head. 'Andres was adamant about that.'

'He thinks of everything, doesn't he?' said Katie.

'You know, I think he does,' Lara agreed.

Sometimes she still couldn't quite believe what was

happening: that she and Andres were falling in love. She had known she was deeply attracted to him almost from the very beginning but she had hardly dared to hope that he might feel the same way about her, especially after his early insistence that he wasn't ready for another relationship. But this feeling between them had seemed to creep up on him and take him unawares, so much so that he seemed totally overwhelmed by the strength of his feelings for her. That he was wooing her in the old-fashioned sense of the word, as she had told Katie, was perfectly true. And as unusual and unexpected as it was, she was determined to enjoy it.

On the day of Cassie's surgery Lara and Dave accompanied her to the Roseberry and stayed there throughout the duration of her operation.

When it was over Andres came to the relatives' room to talk to them, still dressed in his theatre greens. 'It went well,' he said, his gaze moving from Lara to Dave then back to Lara. 'Very well, in fact, and in time, when the swelling has gone down and the wounds have healed, I think Cassie will be pleased with the results.'

'We can't thank you enough,' said Dave, with tears in his eyes.

'Not at all,' Andres replied. 'I'm pleased to be able to help.'

'Can I see her?' asked Dave.

'Of course, but don't tire her. She needs to rest.'

As Dave left the room Lara turned to Andres. 'Thank you,' she whispered. 'Thank you, Andres, from the bottom of my heart.'

Later, after Dave had left to go home to the children, Lara went and sat beside her sister as she recovered. The private room at the Roseberry that had been allocated to Cassie was quiet, tastefully furnished and lit only by a soft lamp beside her bed.

'How are you feeling, Cass?' asked Lara gently as she sat down beside her sister and took her hand.

'Sore,' murmured Cassie from beneath the swathe of dressings that covered her face.

'You're bound to be for a time,' Lara replied, 'but I've spoken to Andres and he said he was very pleased with the way the surgery went and that he hopes that in time you will be delighted at the results.'

'I hope so,' Cassie said. After a moment she went on, 'You know something, Lara? I'm glad Dave wanted to come back while I was still looking so bad because I had thought it was that he couldn't cope with—you know, having a wife who looked like that…'

'Cassie, don't.' Lara gripped her hand more tightly. 'I'm sure his going had nothing to do with that. I just think he reached the end of his tether and became stressed out with all that was happening at that time.'

'I don't suppose my depression helped either,' said Cassie. 'I shut him out, Lara. It was partly my fault.'

'Well, it's all over now. You have your husband back, the children have their father, and Andres has helped to give you a whole new appearance.'

'And you?' said Cassie, suddenly anxious. 'What about you? Are you happy in your new flat?'

'Yes, it's fine,' said Lara. 'You're not to worry about me, Cass. I'm perfectly all right.'

'And what about you and Andres?'

'We're fine, too,' said Lara softly.

'Oh, good,' murmured Cassie sleepily. 'I'm so glad…'

Lara sat and watched her sister as her eyes closed

and she drifted off to sleep. She wasn't sure how long she sat there, recalling all that had happened in the past few weeks since Andres had come into their lives, and how their lives had changed—Cassie's, the children's and her own—and how now, really, nothing would ever be quite the same again.

She was aware of a slight movement behind her then the sound of a voice, a voice that had become so familiar, so instantly recognisable.

'How is she, Lara?'

She turned her head and found him standing slightly behind her.

'She's sleeping,' she answered softly, her heart suffusing with a sudden surge of love for this man who had been responsible for bringing about so much change.

'She needs to rest,' he said. As Lara stood up he took her hand and stood beside her while they both looked down at the sleeping woman in the bed. As they stood there, the emotion of the day suddenly caught up with Lara and the tears that had been threatening for hours welled up in her eyes and spilled over onto her cheeks. Andres, catching sight of her tears, turned her to face him and with his thumbs gently wiped them away.

'I'm sorry,' she choked. 'This is silly of me…'

'Not at all,' he said softly. 'It's been a very emotional time for you.' He slid his arms around her and for a long moment simply held her close while she, after the intense emotion of the day, was quite happy to rest there with her head against his chest.

At last, drawing away a little, he looked into her face. 'Have you eaten?' he asked.

'No.' She shook her head.

'Neither have I,' he replied, 'so I suggest we remedy that right away.'

She was happy for him to take the lead, expecting him to take her to a restaurant or wine bar but feeling a decided sense of relief when instead he instructed the cab driver who collected them from the Roseberry to go straight to his house in Knightsbridge.

Andres prepared a meal for them both, a meal of cold guinea fowl, asparagus, peppers and sun-dried tomatoes, accompanied by a crisp, white Chardonnay and followed by wild strawberries. Afterwards they sat together on the huge white sofa in the sitting room and Andres talked of his home in Argentina.

'I want to take you there someday soon,' he said, one arm protectively around Lara. 'I want you to meet my family and friends. I want to show you the glacier-covered mountains of Patagonia, I want to take you to the Andes and to the very north to show you the Iguacu Falls where thousands of rainbows gleam through the spray…'

'It sounds wonderful,' she breathed, realising for the first time that when he now mentioned his home he no longer talked of Consuela as he had once done.

'It *is* wonderful, my country, the country of my birth,' he agreed. 'Such contrasts of climate and scenery. But you were quite right, my love, about the English countryside on a fine, sunny day—there's nothing quite like it.'

'I'm glad you agree,' she said with a little laugh, then fell silent as he gathered her into his arms. All further conversation between them was replaced by a long kiss that started by being relatively gentle but grew steadily, fuelled by desire and gradually mounting passion.

And when it came to the time when he would usually have suggested taking her home, it seemed the most natural thing in the world that she should stay and that side by side they should go upstairs together.

Not this time did he show her to her own room while he slept in another along the corridor. This time they both went to his room where very slowly he undressed her, lingeringly and lovingly removing each item of her clothing, kissing her skin and caressing her with his fingertips raising her senses to an even more heightened state of arousal until at last he gathered her up into his arms and carried her to the bed. She watched him undress, marvelling at the smooth olive skin and the muscles that rippled across his shoulders, the dark triangle of hair on his chest that tapered to his flat belly and the long lean thighs. Then he was naked and with a deep sigh he joined her, stretching out his long body beside her. He continued to caress her with tongue and fingertips, awakening such longings that she was forced to beg for release.

'You don't like this?' he asked innocently, his dark eyes widening.

'Oh, yes,' she sighed, 'I like it too much.' And when at last they finally made love, their union was everything that Lara could have wished for as with infinite tenderness Andres took her to that mystical place where all reason ceased to exist and where at the moment of tumultuous release, he called her name and told her he loved her. Any lingering doubts she might have had about him being ready for a new relationship were finally swept away.

Later, much later, he held her in his arms and they slept, and when at last in the cold light of dawn Lara woke and turned to the man who still slept by her side, she was overcome with a sense of wonder at the depth of love they had found and the way everything had turned out for everyone. She turned her head again and stared up at the ceiling, remembering that first time she had seen this man from Argentina on that cold January day in his long overcoat and black fedora and how, moments later, she had almost run him over. How terrible it would have been if she had, if she hadn't been able to stop or if he had walked right in front of her car. Little had she dreamt then just how much he would come to mean to her. Her heart filled with love and, turning her head again to look at him, she was surprised to find that during the time she had been thinking about their first meeting, he too had awoken and even now was lying there, watching her.

'You're awake!' she exclaimed softly.

'Yes,' he agreed. 'I was watching you. What were you thinking?'

'I was thinking about the day we met when I almost ran you down, and thanking God that it didn't happen…' Her eyes narrowed slightly. 'But what about you? What were you thinking?'

'I was thinking how lovely you are, how lucky I am to have found you, how I want to spend the rest of my life with you and that I want to make love to you again…right now.'

'How can I argue with any of that?' she said with a little sigh.

'I don't want you to argue,' he murmured as he reached out for her again. 'I just want you to love me.'

MILLS & BOON®

Live the emotion

0405/03b

# Medical romance™

## THE CHILDREN'S HEART SURGEON
***by Meredith Webber*** *(Jimmie's Children's Unit)*

Paediatric heart surgeon Alex Attwood gives all his caring to his tiny patients. He's not interested in women…not since he kissed a blonde stranger long ago and never found her again! So Alex is shocked to meet new nurse manager Annie Talbot. She may have a different name to his mystery woman – but her response to his kiss is the same!

## THE DOCTOR'S LATIN LOVER *by Olivia Gates*
*(24/7)*

When Dr Javier Sandoval Noriega last saw Savannah Richardson he asked her to marry him – and she laughed in his face. So what is the pampered socialite doing in Colombia as part of Javier's Mobile Surgery Unit? Javier can hardly believe it, but he knows he must get rid of her fast – before he falls in love all over again!

## NURSE ON ASSIGNMENT *by Rebecca Lang*

World Aid nurse Lilly Page has gone to Northern Ontario to provide medical aid in the midst of raging forest fires – and to escape her heartache. But it follows her – in the shape of surgeon Rafe Neilson. With danger all around, and emotions running high, can Lilly find the strength to fight her fears and rescue their relationship?

**On sale 6th May 2005**

*Available at most branches of WHSmith, Tesco, ASDA, Martins, Borders, Eason, Sainsbury's and all good paperback bookshops.*

*Visit www.millsandboon.co.uk*